PRAISE FOR G

"Emotional and brilliant…"

"Tastefully erotic … more smart than smutty…"

"Powerful and compelling…"

Originally published by Dreamspinner Press

Second Edition

LUCKY MAN

A HEATED BEAT STORY

GARRETT LEIGH

PROLOGUE

2011

THE LIGHTS dimmed. Smoke filled the stage. The beat of the bass drum sounded, low and deep, like the thud of a steady heart. Danny Jones leaned on the bar, feigning disinterest, but despite his best efforts, no man was immune to the anticipation lacing the air, the kind of anticipation that came with real music… the kind of music that dug out your soul on a Friday night and gave it back to you Saturday afternoon with the mother of all hangovers.

He made his way closer to the stage, pint in hand. The Lamps were the biggest band in the north of England, big enough to draw a capacity crowd to the large local venue—the place was packed. Out of habit Danny scanned the crowd. He spotted a covert drug deal going down a few feet away, and his fingers itched for his warrant card, but he let it go. He'd been looking forward to this gig for weeks, and from the build in noise, he could tell the lights were about to go out. A rush shivered through him. He'd heard the lead singer was hot, but rock stars rarely lived up to the hype. Jim Morrison? Yeah, all right, but the grimy heroin chic of Pete Doherty did nothing for Danny. Nah. He was there for the music.

At least he thought he was until the throaty rumble of Finn McGovern filled his senses, and then it was fair to say he never thought of rock and roll the same way ever again.

CHAPTER ONE

DANNY STARED, transfixed, from his position deep in the crowd. Golden haired, with strong, darkly inked hands, Finn McGovern was bloody gorgeous. And *man*, that voice. Live and untouched by studio wizardry, it was pure, unadulterated magic, and the haunting vocals seeped into Danny's soul.

He absorbed the warm, funky bass line and let the tension from a long week ease out of him. Casework, street work, paperwork. Work, work, bloody work. Danny's week had been hell, but a few songs into the Lamps' set, none of it seemed to matter. Instead he found himself pondering Finn McGovern's blond beard and scruffy leather jacket and the way his black jeans hugged his slim hips. Add in the sultry, gravelly voice, and yeah... Danny was a fucking goner.

"Danny!"

Danny tore his gaze from the stage. His ex-housemate, Kev, loomed into view and dropped a hand on Danny's shoulder.

"Danny, mate. Long time no see. How's tricks? Any hot blokes around for you?"

Danny rolled his eyes as Kev swayed happily beside him. Danny had moved out of the house they shared a month ago, and Kev had banged on his door every week since. "What do you think?"

"Come on. There must be someone here you like."

"Why does there have to be someone I like?"

Kev hiccupped. "Okay, how about someone you just want to bang, then? You need to get *laid*. Even Jackie says so, and you know how she feels about one-night stands."

The last few words were half drowned out by the shouts of the crowd, but Danny got the picture. He was a loser, and even Kev's nicer-than-nice girlfriend thought so.

Great. Danny gave Kev the finger. Kev didn't understand. No one did. Danny had left London with pride and resolution, but over the years, they'd both faded away, and now he was thirty years old, miles from home, and halfway back in the closet.

Danny left Kev and shoved his way to the edge of the crowd. The Lamps gigs were known for getting rowdy, but as much as he liked a good mosh, his exchange with Kev had put a dampener on his mood. He drifted along the fringes, found a spot close to the side of the stage, and stood there awhile, enjoying the dynamic of the band. It was ages before he remembered his glass was empty, and by then Finn McGovern had shed his leather jacket.

Damn, those arms.

Danny pushed through the packed mass of bodies to the bar. He ordered another beer. By the time he turned back to the stage, the band had launched into a rocking song that had the crowd going wild. The growl of the guitars and the crazy beat of the drums pulsated through the crammed venue. Every soul in the building roared the lyrics to a song Danny didn't know, and he knew he stood little chance of muscling his way back to his spot at the side of the stage.

He settled for slouching against the back wall, hoping some distance would break his obsession with the band's rugged lead singer. But it didn't seem to matter how far from the stage Danny stood. Each time he looked up, his pathetic subconscious imagined Finn McGovern was looking right at him, staring through the maddening crowds and singing every line just for him.

Yeah. I really need to get laid.

Eventually the gig played out. The crowd went crazy, and the band came back and played an encore. Their set had been a mixture of their own stuff and covers of well-known crowd pleasers: "Wonderwall," "Song 2," "Common People." Danny expected more of the same for the band's final song, so he was surprised when most of the band sloped off the stage and left Finn McGovern alone with his acoustic guitar for company.

"All right, folks. Let's slow this down. Say good-bye the old fashioned way."

The lights dimmed, low and intimate. Finn McGovern strummed a few chords. Danny recognized them immediately, and if he hadn't been so bewitched by the singer's deep northern accent, he would've melted to the floor. "Lucky Man." The Verve. *Is he trying to kill me?*

A LITTLE while later, Danny found himself alone at the bar. Most of the crowd had dissipated and disappeared into the surrounding local pubs, Kev and his bird included, but Danny didn't feel like going with the flow. He felt too mellow to brave the chaos of a Saturday night high street. Finn McGovern's solo rendition of Danny's favorite song had blown his mind, and he wanted to sit awhile and bask in its resonance. Who cared if he was the only soul at the deserted bar?

Not Danny. In some ways the lonely afterglow of an awesome gig was the best part. Danny usually enjoyed it at home, lying alone in his bed, staring at the ceiling with whatever band he'd seen still ringing in his ears. Not tonight, though. Tonight he couldn't be arsed to find a taxi. Not yet.

And he wasn't drunk enough to sidle on home by himself either, so he ditched the pints and got himself a whiskey and Coke. No ice. Just lemon. It slid down in a flash, so he bought another and another. He was quite happily lashed off his face by the time a familiar voice broke through his drunken haze.

"Can I buy you a drink?"

Danny glanced up and then looked behind him.

Finn McGovern laughed. "Daft twat. Yeah, I mean *you*."

"Um, sure." *Smooth. Idiot.* Danny gave himself an internal shake. "I mean, yeah, thanks. Grouse and Coke."

Like magic Danny's drink appeared in front of him. Minus ice, with added lemon.

Finn McGovern put his own shot of something dangerous and clear on the bar and pulled up a stool. "You were at the gig tonight, right? At the back, by the wall?"

"How do you know that?"

"I had the best view. I'm Finn. Nice to meet you."

Finn held out his hand. Danny took it, feeling a little like he'd dropped into the twilight zone. "Danny."

"Danny." Finn repeated the name like it pleased him, and his lazy smile widened. "I've never seen you in the crowd before. Is this the first gig you've been to?"

Danny wondered how Finn had read him so easily. "I've got your EP, but I've never seen you live before. My mate Kev dragged me along tonight."

"Dragged, eh? Now there's an endorsement."

Danny met Finn's smirk with a grin of his own. "I didn't mean it like that. I wasn't going to come out tonight. Didn't feel like it."

"So…." Finn shifted on his stool. He put his elbows on the bar and leaned forward. In the dim light of the deserted venue, Danny could see his eyes were a rich caramel brown flecked with gold. Laughter lines swept upward, and combined with the stubbly growth on his jaw, he looked a few years younger than Danny. "Who are you here with?"

Danny glanced around at the near-empty venue, then shot

Finn a wry look. "No one, now. I came with Kev and his girl, but they left."

"Shame. Did they enjoy the gig?"

"I think everyone enjoyed the gig." Danny's words were honest and heartfelt, and the grin that lit up Finn's face did funny things to Danny's bones. Made them warm and feel like jelly, which was an odd combination. "I didn't know you played the Verve covers. If I'd known that, I'd have come to a show a lot sooner."

Finn stretched his arms over his head. Danny could see that though he was buzzed from the gig, he was tired too. He had to be. Finn hadn't strayed far from his microphone stand, but he'd put everything he had into every chord and note. "*Urban Hymns* is my desert island album. The guys think their stuff is a bit morbid for big venues like this, though."

"Didn't stop you at the end," Danny mused, remembering the spine-tingling rendition of "Lucky Man."

"Yeah, well. I love that song. And it always strikes a chord with me when I look out over a crowd and see them connecting with what we do. It sounds corny but it's true. It's about more than folks getting shitfaced and having a mosh."

Danny smiled. Finn's expression was so earnest that he would've been convinced no matter the depth of sincerity to his words. Then he took a moment to pinch himself. Finn's voice was as entrancing now as it had been when he was singing to the masses. Was this really happening?

Maybe not. Maybe someone had slipped something into his drink and he was imagining the whole thing. But who cared? The scent of beer and sweat mixed with something that must've been uniquely Finn McGovern clouded his brain, and for the next hour or so, the rest of the world faded away.

It was two in the morning by the time Finn put his hand on Danny's arm. "So you said you didn't want to come out. How do you feel now? Glad you came?"

Danny stared at the inked hand on his arm. It was

November and pissing with icy rain outside, but Finn's palm felt scorching, like it was the first hand to ever touch Danny's skin. *He's not flirting. He's not flirting. Rock stars are straight... like coppers, right? Shit, I'm so fucked up.* "I… uh, had a great night. Where's the rest of your band?"

Finn let his hand drop, and the tension in the air faded a little. "Most of them are across the road. They like to go and get pissed with the fans after a gig."

"You don't?"

Finn shrugged. "I *love* talking about the gig, but I don't like crowds. A busy pub on a Saturday night is my idea of hell."

Danny raised an eyebrow, curious in spite of the party his nerves were having in his gut. "How does that work for you on stage?"

"That's different." Finn downed the last of his drink. "On stage I forget about everyone else, but after, when everyone wants a piece of me, it gets a bit much. I don't know who to look at first, you know?"

Danny didn't. Finn's logic made sense, but in Danny's line of work, shit like that didn't matter. He just had to get on with it. "Won't they wonder where you are?"

"Maybe." Finn slid his stool a little closer. Close enough so his denim-clad thigh touched Danny's. "But I'll just tell them I went home with the hottest guy at the gig tonight."

CHAPTER TWO

THEY STUMBLED through Finn's front door. His house was closer to the venue than Danny's, and after a frenzied encounter in the car park, it seemed the sensible option.

Finn kicked the door shut. The bang startled Danny. He could hardly remember the cab ride across town, and the dark, still quiet of Finn's hallway took him by surprise. Suddenly Finn *did* seem real. Real and breathing hard, his face flushed, lips swollen from Danny's kiss. Finn kissed Danny again, and Danny's head spun. Much of the evening had seemed a dream, but this most of all: Touching Finn. Kissing Finn. Any minute now he was going to wake up.

"Do you want a drink?" Finn touched Danny's face. The gesture was softer than any they'd shared so far.

Danny shook his head. He'd drunk more than enough, though he knew the bellyful of whiskey took most of the credit for giving him the balls to crawl into the backseat of a taxi behind Finn. "I'm good. Thanks."

Finn grinned and inclined his head toward the stairs. "Me too. Want to come up?"

As if Danny was going to refuse. He left his shoes beside Finn's rock star biker boots and followed Finn upstairs. On the landing, Finn yanked him into the nearest room. Danny didn't have time to wonder if it was actually Finn's bedroom before Finn was on him again.

Danny let Finn push him into the door and fell slack as Finn tore at his clothes with guitar-calloused hands and unbuckled his belt. Returning the favor felt natural, like it hadn't been more than a year since he'd last touched a man. He shoved his hands under Finn's T-shirt and found hard, unyielding flesh that coiled like wire and jumped beneath his searching fingertips.

Finn groaned into Danny's mouth. "I've been thinking about this since the lights went up and I saw you staring at me."

"I don't believe you." Danny punctuated the words with kisses on Finn's arched throat. "It was dark, full of people, and you had your eyes closed when you started playing. You couldn't have seen me."

Finn chuckled and pushed Danny's jeans over his hips. "Okay, you've rumbled me. Maybe I was watching the crowd before the show started. Maybe I saw you come in with your mates."

"You saw me come in?"

"Better than that." Finn kicked Danny's jeans away and pulled his T-shirt over his head. "I saw you get off the bus. I was looking out the window, hoping you'd cross the road and come to the show. I couldn't believe my luck when I saw you in the crowd." Finn did away with his own T-shirt without waiting for Danny to recover his power of speech. "Wow. You're even hotter without clothes."

Heat flooded Danny's cheeks. With his eclectic mix of Welsh and Chinese genes, he knew he was fairly inter-esting to look at, but as he absorbed Finn's leonine beauty, he couldn't help averting his gaze. The last bloke he'd slept with had been gone by morning, and they'd never got round to exchanging names. Finn's wide-eyed stare got under his skin, and he didn't know where to look.

Get a grip, dickhead. You can face busting the door of a crack den, but not this?

Finn caught Danny's chin as he looked down. "Oh no you don't. You're fit as fuck. Don't be ashamed of it."

Danny stared. The room was dark, but Danny could see the outline of Finn's cock bulging in his jeans, and his own dick ached with long-neglected need. "You're gorgeous too."

Finn smiled and released Danny's chin. He took a few steps back and sank onto a double bed. "Come here and fuck me, then."

Danny blinked, frozen for a moment. He was versatile, but given Finn's dominance until that moment, he'd assumed *he* would be the one getting fucked. He cast his gaze over Finn again and a thrill ran through him. Finn McGovern was the guy every man dreamed of sliding inside. Body hair, tattoos, and a scruffy beard—he was the stuff of fantasies. At least Danny's fantasies. "Are you sure?"

Finn reached into a bedside drawer and tossed him a box of condoms. "I'm sure."

Okay, then. Danny's nerves and apprehension evaporated. He crossed the room in two strides and grasped Finn's jeans. He made short work of yanking them down Finn's legs, and it wasn't long before their remaining clothes became a forgotten pile on the floor.

The air shifted then. Danny kissed every inch of Finn he could reach: His throat. His chest. The line of golden hair that led to his groin. Finn smelled amazing, like clean sweat, smoke, and pine needles. Like Danny imagined a naked man in a forest would smell like. He was responsive too, more so than any man Danny had ever been with before, and his throaty grunts and growls went straight to Danny's dick.

Danny covered Finn, grinding their cocks together. Finn dug his fingers into Danny's back and arched his body. Their lips met in another bruising kiss, a kiss that went on and on until Finn broke away.

"Man, come *on*. I'm bloody shaking here."

Danny looked down and saw Finn was indeed trembling. The sight, though one of the hottest things he'd ever seen, threw him. Was Finn scared? Or did he really want *Danny* that much? Either way, Danny shivered, and anticipation rolled through him. He squeezed some lube on his fingers. Finn scooted back on the bed and raised his legs. Danny slipped a cautious finger into him and the world stopped. Danny circled his fingers and stretched Finn, absorbing his sharp gasps until Finn stilled his hand.

"Enough. I'm ready."

Danny rolled a condom on, lubed up, and spread some extra lube on Finn's dick for good measure. Finn shuddered and bucked into Danny's touch. His eyes fluttered closed. Danny had never seen anything like it. He rose up on his knees and grasped Finn's strong thighs, raising them, and parted them enough to slot in between them. Then he eased inside Finn, smooth warmth enveloped him, and for the second time that night, his head spun. The urgency between them had faded a little while they'd taken the necessary precautions, but it was back now full force, and it was all Danny could do not to cram himself inside Finn and pound him for the three seconds it would take to blow his load.

But he didn't. He moved with care, testing the waters as Finn braced himself against the headboard and raised himself from the mattress. Finn rolled his pelvis in time with Danny's thrusts, and the sight of Finn's stomach muscles rippling with every pulsing circle of his hips just about did Danny in. He hadn't topped in forever, and Finn blew apart his memories of the last time he'd felt the tight, hot heat of a man clamped around his dick.

Danny dropped his palms to the bed and overrode Finn's movements with a series of jabbing thrusts.

Finn's mouth fell open and his eyes rolled. "Oh fuck, yeah."

Encouraged, Danny moved faster, harder, fucking into Finn until he found a rhythm that made them both groan.

Finn wrapped his long legs around Danny's body. Their contrasting skin looked good together... *so* good.

Danny growled. Finn tugged on Danny's hair and threw his head back. The arch of his throat was too alluring to ignore. Danny fused his lips to Finn's Adam's apple and swirled his tongue in gentle contrast to the punishing roll of his hips.

The gesture was Finn's undoing. Harsh breaths mingled with grunts and moans until his heady sounds cut off. He arched his back and closed his inked hand around his cock. "Gonna bust."

The words had barely left Finn's mouth before he came, and Danny stared in wonder, watching and feeling as Finn's body tightened and flexed. He watched the flush on Finn's chest break out with sweat. Watched the vein in his neck pulse. Watched him pump his dick until he spilled on his own belly.

Danny slowed his pace. Finn dug his fingers into Danny's thighs. "Keep fucking me. You're close. I can feel it."

So could Danny. He grabbed the headboard and slammed into Finn. The bed groaned in protest, but Finn urged him on, his lips at Danny's ear, raking his nails down Danny's back.

Danny couldn't take it for long. He came with Finn whispering dirty things in his ear, his mouth open and slack in a silent scream.

He fell to the side and collapsed in a sweaty heap. His arms burned and ached from the effort of holding himself up, and he felt utterly boneless. *Wow.*

Somewhere beside him, Finn let out a rumbly moan. "Wow."

"Yeah."

Finn chuckled. "I wasn't even sure you were gay. Guess I know now. Can't believe I pulled a bloke as fit as you."

Danny laughed too, though it was muffled by whatever he'd mashed his face into. "You're the bloody rock star."

"You're joking, right?" Finn yanked the pillow from

beneath Danny and forced him to look up. "You're way hotter than me."

Argument bubbled up Danny's chest, but the need to dispose of the sticky condom and clean up made itself known. "Keep dreaming, mate. Got a towel?"

Finn fell back on the bed and flung his arm vaguely toward the door. "Bathroom is second on the left. Don't worry. There's no one else here."

Danny crept across the landing anyway. The whole world could've come home to Finn's house while they'd been fucking and he wouldn't have noticed. He chucked the condom, cleaned himself up, and grabbed a flannel for Finn. When he got back, Finn wiped himself down and crawled into bed. Danny looked around for his clothes, taking his dismissal.

"What are you doing?"

"Um, looking for my clothes?" Danny didn't know why he'd answered a question with a question. Finn seemed to have that effect on him.

"What do you need clothes for?" Finn held up the duvet. "Get in."

Danny woke with his face smushed between Finn's shoulder blades and his arms tight around Finn. Their positioning felt natural, like they slept together all the time, and it took Danny a moment to remember he was wrapped around a man he'd only known a matter of hours.

He pulled back, his bladder aching even more than his pounding head. At some point in the night he'd heard Finn's housemate come home, so he dressed in the first clothes he found on the floor and tiptoed across the landing to take a leak.

When he got back he realized he'd pulled on Finn's T-shirt. It smelled of him... of rock-star sweat and smoke machines. Danny considered making a dash for home still wearing it… keeping it as a reminder of the best sex he'd had in years, but with Finn's housemate banging around downstairs, he didn't feel like doing the walk of shame just yet.

Instead he entertained himself poking around Finn's room while Finn slept on, searching for clues about the man who'd surprised him so much the night before.

Yeah. That's right. Danny still couldn't quite believe he'd fucked Finn McGovern.

He wandered around peering at photographs and picking up this and that. Ornaments. Books. An ashtray made from seashells. That piqued Danny's curiosity. He knew from their alcohol-fueled conversation last night that Finn didn't smoke, and that had surprised him. His gravelly voice put an image of a chain-smoking lout in Danny's mind, but in reality there was far more to Finn than a stale cliché.

He moved on. The room was large, typical of Victorian townhouses, with a high ceiling and a big bay window. It even had an unused fireplace, complete with a mock fire that seemed to be built entirely from drumsticks.

That made Danny smile. Finn's music was everywhere he looked—guitars, vinyl records, concert photographs. There was even a small electric piano in the corner by the window. Danny pressed a few keys, tracing out a rough version of a classical piece he'd once known. He hadn't played in years, and he'd never been particularly good.

"Do you play?"

Danny jumped and glanced over his shoulder. Finn was sitting up, rubbing his eyes, disheveled and gorgeous. "Not really. My nan taught me some when I was little, but I've forgotten it all now."

Finn shrugged and slid from the bed, nude. He drifted off to the bathroom like he walked around naked all the time. Maybe he did.

The front door slammed. Danny looked around for his

clothes. He was yanking his jeans up his legs when Finn came back in the room and sat on the edge of the bed.

"Where are you going?"

"Home."

"Got stuff to do?"

"Not really." He had just come off a week of night shifts. He was free as a bird until Tuesday morning.

"People to see?"

"Nope."

A faint smile played at Finn's lips. "Then come back to bed."

Danny deliberated only a moment. It was almost too easy to let Finn undress him and coax him back under the covers. Again Finn knew exactly what he wanted. He rolled onto his stomach and tugged Danny over him. Danny covered him and fucked him slow and deep, transfixed by their clasped hands and Finn's low cries of pleasure. It wasn't the fantasies he'd dreamed when he'd been alone late at night, in his flat, or working the mean streets of Nottingham. It was better.

After, Finn stretched out beside Danny and rubbed his belly. "Man, I'm so hungover. I need a nap and a roast dinner."

"You just woke up."

"Hmm. Well, you wore me out."

"Takes two to tango." Danny let his eyes drift closed. The sex had been sweet and intense, and he was still basking in the afterglow.

Finn hummed again and traced patterns on Danny's forearm with his rough fingertips. He said no more, and it wasn't long before they both dozed off.

Danny woke a little while later to find Finn wide-awake and entirely serious about the need for a good roast dinner.

"We could go to the White Horse. It's quiet and they do wicked Yorkies in there."

Danny hesitated. Just because he hadn't known Finn was gay, that didn't mean no one else did. He rubbed Finn's silky hair between his fingertips, hiding his indecision with a kiss. "We could stay in and I could make you one?"

The compromise seemed to make Finn's bright smile wider than ever. "Really? Homemade?"

Danny let Finn's good humor seep into him. A night on the beer had given him a raging headache, but the light in Finn's face made him feel warm. "I can do a mean roast chicken."

Finn pounced on him, rolling him around the bed like they'd been lovers for years. Danny pulled away for air. "What about your housemate?"

"Jack? Nah, he went to his boyfriend's this morning, and then he's off to Berlin for the week. Won't be back till Friday."

"Berlin?"

"Yeah. Jack's a DJ. Beat Jak. Ever heard of him?"

"Nope." Danny tucked a stray lock of hair behind Finn's ear. "So you've got the place all to yourself?"

"Yep." Finn kissed Danny again, but with them both recently satisfied and fairly hungover, it wasn't long before Danny found himself borrowing Finn's shower and schlepping down the road to the local Tesco Express.

After an afternoon of cooking, kissing, and… other stuff, bodging a full roast with a perfect stranger turned out to be the best idea he'd ever had.

CHAPTER THREE

FINN MCGOVERN tucked his Gibson into her case and stretched his arms over his head. It had been a long day. His shoulders ached and his fingers were sore, but in spite of an ill-advised weekend on the beer, he felt good… really good. The kind of good that only came from an epic studio session or a mind-blowing fuck, and in recent days, he'd had both.

He packed up the rest of his gear, making small talk with his fellow musicians, but his mind was elsewhere, like it had been all day, back at home, watching over the inky-haired streak of muscle he'd left in his bed that morning. He wondered if Danny would still be there when he got home. The bloke had proved a bit of an enigma, and after a weekend spent mostly in bed, Finn had crept away from him with the sense that he was about to fall headfirst into something crazy.

Even crazier than you….

Finn drove home hoping that, for once, he was right, but it wasn't to be. There was no sign of Danny, and the empty house felt like a sinking stone in the pit of his stomach. Crowded places freaked him out, but being all alone in the big old house did his head in just as much. Without another presence to guide him, he rarely felt sure what was real and what was just his malfunctioning imagination.

And that was without the sight of his stripped bed.

It's like he was never here.

Finn pushed the thought away and went in search of his bedsheets. He found them in the tumble dryer, warm and clean, and mourned the loss of his Danny-scented bed. To cheer himself up, he ordered a pizza and spent the evening watching *Spartacus* and messing around on the guitar. He was halfway through a mental list of the Verve's back catalogue when his phone rang.

He dove for it, hoping it would be Danny, but it was Jack, calling from Berlin to check in. Finn rolled his eyes. He'd been renting his spare room to Jack for the past two years, and he was still getting used to having a roommate who gave a shit. He answered the call with a rueful grin. "All right, mate? How's Germany?"

Jack sighed. "German. And cold. And wet. I swear this place gets more bloody British each time I'm here."

Finn snorted, though he felt bad for Jack. Jack loved his work, but he hated being away from his partner, and traveling always put him in a bad mood. "I fed your fish, if that's why you're calling."

Jack had the good grace to laugh. "Yeah, you've caught me out. You know I can't sleep unless they've had their dinner. Seriously, though. I saw you hitting the beer at the weekend, so I wondered…."

The sentence hung between them like a dark cloud. Jack knew Finn well… too well. "I know, I know. I just felt like being a normal bloke for once. Think I got away with it."

"And the rest?"

Finn scowled. Danny and Jack hadn't crossed paths, but he knew Jack would've noticed the extra pair of shoes by the door. The notion irked Finn. Until that moment his time with Danny had felt like a precious secret, untainted by the real world. "Don't start. How often do I have to listen to you and Will shagging?"

"I'm not complaining, mate. Just curious. You never let anyone stay the night."

Finn shrugged before he remembered Jack couldn't see him. Jack's statement was kind. Finn never let anyone stay because he never brought anyone home. Never wanted to. Home was his sacred place… his safe place, when he wasn't climbing the walls by himself. "He was nice."

"Did you tell him?"

"Yeah, I rolled over right after he fucked me and said, hey, guess what? I'm a fucking—"

"All right, all right." Jack cut in before Finn could get truly annoyed. "I'm sorry, okay? I just want you to be happy."

Finn's grunt was noncommittal, but Jack let it go. They were good friends… good enough to know when an awkward conversation had run its course. Jack rang off after reminding Finn to keep an appointment that had been stuck to the fridge door since the beginning of the month—an appointment Finn was hardly likely to forget.

Still, he drifted to the kitchen to check it anyway. Paranoia was a lifestyle choice. Why worry when he could just fucking look? And there it was: *Monday 2:30 p.m. Nurse Stutby*. Same as it was every bloody month.

Finn started to turn away. An out-of-place card stopped him in his tracks. He frowned and plucked it from the fridge door. The nondescript business card had nothing but a mobile number printed on it, and was probably Jack's, but Finn hadn't seen it before, he was sure of it, wasn't he?

Finn turned the card over and over, searching for a clue that wasn't there. The logical side of his brain slowed to a crawl like it always did when doubt clouded his mind. If the number was meant for Jack, it had been there for twenty-four hours, and Finn would've seen it that morning or even the night before. True, he'd been distracted by an extended one-night—*two*-night—stand, but the card was white… and almost all of Jack's music contacts used funky black cards. A tiny detail, but Finn had learned the hard way the small things mattered.

He took the intriguing card upstairs and left it on the bedside table while he remade his bed. It taunted him. He stared at it for far too long before he turned his back on it and stomped off to the shower.

It was still there when he came back, towel around his waist, hair dripping. He skirted around it, averting his gaze while he dried off and pulled on a pair of softly worn jogging bottoms, but when he slid into his empty bed, his resolve ran out.

He turned out the lights and lay down. He'd often found his nerves less potent in the dark. He punched the number in and waited for it to ring, figuring he'd hang up if the voice at the other end wasn't the one he wanted to hear. Irony struck him. How many times had he done just that? Turned his back on the wrong kind of voice?

Too many to count. He closed his eyes and searched for his happy place. For once he didn't have to look too far….

"You missed a bit."

"Hmm?" Danny glanced up from the sudsy sink. Since their late lunch, he'd seemed in a world of his own.

"The tin. Look."

Danny frowned at the grease-streaked roasting tin. "Is this where you sing me a line from the Fairy Liquid advert?"

"I'm not drunk enough for that game anymore." Finn leaned over Danny's shoulder and pressed their cheeks together. Danny felt warm and solid, and though he sensed Danny was gearing up to leave, he didn't want to let go. "Still beat you, though."

Danny chuckled. He'd tried to catch Finn out all the way home from the gig the night before, but to no avail. Sad but true: Finn knew the theme song from every cheesy ad Danny could think of. "I want a rematch."

"Yeah?"

"Yeah." Danny rinsed the last dish and handed it over.

Finn shoved it in the cupboard with little care, noting Danny's gaze sliding to the clock on the microwave. "Got somewhere to be?

"What? Oh no… not really. Just figured it was getting late." Danny turned and pulled Finn against him. The embrace felt casual and easy… too easy. Finn sighed and kissed Danny's neck, and for the third time since they'd met, he convinced Danny to slope back upstairs and fall into his bed….

"Hello?"

Finn jumped. His mind had wandered too far, and he'd forgotten what he'd been waiting for, but there was no denying the flat, bored tone was a poor incarnation of the voice he'd been daydreaming about all day. "Danny? That you?"

"Yeah. Who's that… shit, hang on." Rustling. A car door slamming, then Danny came back on the line. "Finn?"

"It's me."

"Sorry, mate. I was driving. How're you doing? Long time no speak."

Finn laughed and relaxed. *See? Wasn't so hard, was it?* "I think we last spoke at 2:00 a.m."

"Yeah? What did we talk about?"

Finn felt warm all over. Danny hadn't seemed the type to talk dirty over the phone, but perhaps he'd misjudged him, which wasn't hard to believe. Even naked and moving over Finn, Danny had proved a bit of an enigma. He'd seemed unsure of himself at first, especially when he'd taken his clothes off, but there was something about him… a strength, an edge that told Finn there was far more to the quiet man than met the eye. "You sound miles away. Did you emigrate Down Under since I last saw you?"

"Even if I had, I wouldn't have got there yet. I'd be in… I don't know, Singapore, maybe?"

Finn laughed again. "So… where are you?"

"I just got home."

"Where's that?" Finn pushed his luck. "You didn't tell me

much yesterday. You could be a reggae dancer from Timbuktu for all I know."

"Would that be bad?"

"No, just unexpected. You don't look like much of a dancer."

Danny snorted. "You've got me there. I can't dance for shit. I'm a… policeman, actually. And I live at the bottom of Marsden Heights."

Finn heard Danny's hesitation like a fucking siren. Policeman. Wow. That explained a lot. "Marsden Heights? In the flats?"

"Yep. Top floor."

Finn hummed and turned it all over in his mind. "You don't look like a copper. You're not old enough."

"Don't you start. I get that from cons all the time."

"Maybe they fancy you."

Danny laughed. "Hope not. I work Vice."

A pause stretched out between them, an awkward silence that hadn't been there the day before. Finn wondered if this was what happened when one-night stands went on too long, so he broke it first. He'd called Danny for a reason, right? "So… I'm not gigging this weekend. Do you want to grab a curry or something?"

"I'm working all weekend, but I get off shift at ten on Saturday. That too late for you?"

"No, it's perfect, actually. I've got a jam session in the city that will probably go on late. Have you been to Moja before?"

"That all-night dive behind the coach park?"

Finn rolled his eyes. "It's not a dive. It's a canteen and it's awesome. What do you say?"

Danny was silent a moment, deliberating. Finn wondered what he was doing, what his flat looked like. You could tell a lot about a man by the way he kept his home. In the darkness Finn's gaze fell on the fire he'd built out of Jack's discarded drumsticks. *Yeah? So he probably already knows you're a nutjob….*

23

"Finn? You there?"

Finn felt a flutter in his stomach, and the endearing hint of uncertainty in Danny's voice made it worse. "Sorry. What were you saying?"

"I said you've got yourself a deal. See you Saturday."

CHAPTER FOUR

THE NEXT six days crawled by. Danny couldn't get Finn out of his head and found himself preoccupied even at work… especially at work, where he didn't have time for distractions.

Danny eyed the paperwork on his desk. Like most aspects of his life, it was stacked into orderly piles—neat, clinical, nothing out of place—but something was irking him, something that overrode even his fixation with a certain blond rock star. Danny opened a file and flipped through a few pages. The haggard faces of Nottingham's prostitutes stared back at him, all with neatly written notes beneath them cataloguing their known habits and stomping grounds. Danny's colleagues often laughed at him for his meticulous records, but he didn't care. How would you notice something amiss if you didn't know what it had been like to begin with? And on Danny's patch, something had definitely changed: the dynamic; the vibe; the footfall. Something was off.

"Evening, Danny. Got a minute?"

Danny glanced up. Somehow he'd missed his boss, DCI Brown, taking a seat on the edge of his desk. "Guv?"

"Memo from Greater Manchester. Thought it might be of interest to you."

"Yeah?" Danny scanned the e-mail detailing a spate of

missing prostitutes, five in total. The link between them all was tenuous at present, but detectives working the case were concerned enough to alert every force in the country. "That's a lot of missing persons."

"Certainly is. Have you noticed anything? Any toms you're worried about? Girls gone walkabout?"

Danny shrugged. As the newbie on the squad, his main role was the job no one wanted: monitoring the welfare of the city's toms—the sex workers. An impossible task when the department as a whole had been charged with running them off the streets. How could he observe what he couldn't see?

But that was a debate for another day. As far as the DCI's question was concerned, there wasn't much Danny could say. Toms disappeared off his patch all the time, lost to drugs, trafficking, and God knew what else, and despite his anal approach to record keeping, Danny couldn't keep track of them all. "I've got a few snouts I can ask. In fact there's a source I've been meaning to touch base with for a while. I'll head out tonight."

"Good idea. Take Bob with you. Get the old goat some fresh air."

The DCI retrieved his briefcase from the floor, shrugged into his coat, and bid Danny good night, done for the day while Danny was on shift until dawn.

Danny glared after his retreating back. He wasn't in the mood for company, at least not the kind Bob Jenkins had to offer. Bob was an old-school copper—conditioned to bust easy collars and wait for the real trouble to fall into his lap—and he'd made his opinion on Danny's "newfangled" methods well known.

An hour later, parked up in the city's red-light district, he was still making them known.

"This is a waste of time. Let's go down Trinity Street and do a curb sweep."

Danny scowled. Busting johns for curb crawling did nothing but push the toms further into an underworld that was much harder to police, a world of poorly lit streets and dark alleys where Danny was as likely to come across a body as he was a crime. "Not yet. My snout doesn't stick her head up till late. Give her a bit longer."

Bob grumbled under his breath but for once let Danny have his way. "Fine, but I'm not driving around this shithole all night. If she ain't there, we're heading back to the factory to finish that paperwork from that bollocks pimp bust you roped me into last week. Bloody youngbloods. Think you know it all."

Danny rolled his eyes. He *was* young to be a vice-squad detective, but he'd worked hard, slogged his way through uni and two years on the beat in Brixton before he'd made the jump to CID. He'd earned his place, and Bob knew it.

And as luck would have it, Danny's informant appeared on the streets just as he was running out of excuses to wait around for her.

Danny left Bob in the car and approached the street corner, head down, low profile, until he was close enough to call out without attracting unwanted attention. "Hey, Lexi. How's tricks?"

"Well, well, well. If it isn't my favorite copper." Lexi loomed out of the shadows and huffed a cloud of weed smoke into the frosty night air. "Come to smack my wrist for my dirty habits?"

"Maybe. Got anything juicy to distract me with?"

"Like what?"

Danny shrugged and leaned against a lamppost, half an eye trained on the hollow faces around them, watching for lurking pimps and creeping cars. "Anything. Everything. Where's Netty at? Haven't seen her around for a while."

"She went to Birmingham with her fella." Lexi flicked her spent joint into the gutter. "Reckoned she was getting clean. Believe it when I see it."

"Why would you see it if she got clean, eh? Not like she'd come back here, is it?"

27

Danny had Lexi there. The streets were no place for an ex-tom. If Netty really was clean, chances were neither of them would ever hear of her again.

If only. Danny knew of only one girl who'd escaped the life of hooking and junk, and she'd had a damned sight more going for her than any of the women he'd seen in recent months. "What about Jeanie? She still working this patch?"

Lexi spat on the ground. "You probably know better than me."

"Try me." Danny took another glance around. He was running out of time. Chatting Lexi up much longer would bring trouble for both of them. "What about Terry, Brandy, and Ebony? Anyone you haven't seen for a while? Anyone you're worried about?"

Lexi eyed Danny as sharply as her clouded gaze allowed. "Why are you asking me that?"

"Why not?" Danny pushed off the lamppost and started to turn away. "Do you still have my card?"

"Feeling lonely, DC Jones?"

"Do you have it or not?"

Lexi sighed. "Can't blame a gal for trying, and yeah, I still have it, pinned to my bedroom wall."

Danny chanced a rueful grin over his shoulder. "Good girl. Give me a call if your mates don't show up, okay?"

He walked away without waiting for an answer. Lexi wouldn't call him, but with any luck, she'd remember the conversation and take notice if the faces around her began to disappear. It wasn't much, but it was better than nothing.

DANNY WIPED his sweaty palms on his jeans. He spent more time than he cared to admit parked up outside questionable establishments, but this was the first time in as long as he could remember he'd felt so damned fucking nervous.

Man up. It's just a bloody curry.

But was it? Really? Part of Danny hoped so, but then the other, louder side of him wanted it to be far more than *just* anything. Wanted… needed to know the magical thirty-six hours he'd spent with Finn McGovern had been real. Danny's memories were enough to leave him breathless, but what if he was wrong? What if Finn wasn't as hot or quietly charismatic as Danny remembered? Or worse? What if Finn's beer goggles had been faulty too? What if Finn took one look at him sober and cringed?

Would serve you bloody right, daft idiot.

Danny got out of the car with a wry smirk. He hadn't been on a date in years, and there was only one way to find out if Finn was as gorgeous as he remembered.

The curry house Finn had texted him directions to was in a dodgy part of the city, close to the motorway, but Danny was used to that, used to blending in with his trainers, worn jeans, and scruffy coat. He debated leaving the coat in the car, but it was too bloody cold for vanity. He pulled his collar up against the wind and looked up and down the street. There was no one about save a pisshead leaning on a phone box and a group of young lads loading a van.

He headed in the direction of the van. He got closer and saw the pavement stacked with guitar cases and half a drum kit. He thought of Finn—as if he wasn't already—and wondered if they were part of the jam session he'd come from. As Danny passed them, a more southern accent than he was used to cut through the broad northern brogues.

"…good to see Finn smiling again, wasn't it? It's been too long, man…."

At least Danny thought that's what he heard. By the time he was a few feet away, he felt less convinced. He glanced over his shoulder and the pavement was clear, the van door shut, leaving him no way of knowing who'd said it, if indeed anyone had said it at all.

Idiot. He had Finn on the brain. *Finn brain.* Danny chuckled. Despite the churning nerves in his gut, he kind of liked the sound of that.

The all-night Indian café was quiet, as Finn had promised. Danny absorbed the steamy warmth and searched the booths. It didn't take long to spot Finn's shaggy blond hair, and Danny's heart did a little flip. Damn. Finn McGovern *was* as gorgeous as Danny remembered, and more… head down, scribbling in a notebook, chewing his thumbnail, oblivious to Danny's presence.

"You going in or what, mate?"

"Hmm?" Danny shook himself and sidestepped the grumpy old geezer and then wove his way through the small hole-in-the-wall restaurant to where Finn sat. "All right?"

Finn looked up and beamed, wide and warm. "Hey, you. Yeah, I'm all right. How are you?"

"Good, good." Danny dropped into his seat, trying not to grin like an idiot. "Not sure about this place, though. Looks like it's got rats."

Finn's mile-wide smile turned to a smirk as he stuffed his notebook into his guitar case. "You'll see."

A waiter came before Danny could reply. They ordered drinks and papadums. Danny asked for a lager and Finn another bottle of water to replace the empty one on the table.

"Are you driving?" Danny asked when the waiter was gone.

Finn shrugged. "I don't drink much. It's not good for me."

"Bad for your voice?"

"Something like that."

The waiter delivered a tray of papadums and pickles. Danny hadn't looked at the menu, too busy gawping at Finn, so he ordered the first thing he saw along with a few side dishes.

Finn chuckled and added to their mammoth order. "Didn't have you pegged for a madras kind of man."

"Yeah?" Danny waited for the waiter to go. "What *did* you have me pegged for? A korma wimp?"

"Other way, actually. Thought you'd be a hotter-the-better bloke."

A rude joke danced on Danny's tongue until he remembered he was sober and out in public.

Out in public with a guy half the city probably recognizes….

Danny silenced the devil on his shoulder. "I lived behind a curry house at uni. Opened my eyes to a whole new world. I grew up on chop suey and cawl."

And the rest. University had been Danny's first real taste of sexual freedom. Something that felt a world away these days.

"Cawl?" Finn frowned. "I get the Chinese reference, your eyes give you away, but what's the other shit?"

"Welsh. I was born in Cardiff. My mum did most of the cooking, but my dad used to make cawl on Saturdays. It's like broth… Irish stew without the barley."

Finn looked mystified. Danny let it go. "How was your jam? Was it a Lamps thing?"

"Nah." Finn cracked a papadum in half. "I work as a session musician for a couple of bands. We're hitting the recording studio next week, so we needed to touch base."

"A session musician?" That caught Danny off guard. The Lamps were a big deal. They sold out every venue they played, especially up north. Danny had figured they had it made. "Thought you'd be making the big bucks by now."

"I am, as much as I need to." Finn's gaze was steady, but Danny felt like he was missing something.

"So why do you play for other bands?"

"The Lamps don't have a record deal. We're independent."

Danny swallowed a mouthful of warm lager. Blah. He hoped the food was better than the beer. "Hard to get signed?"

"Don't want to get signed." Finn stirred some DayGlo-pink coconut into an amber pool of mango chutney. "We're happy as we are. None of us do it for the money."

"Really?" Danny winced at his own skepticism, but it was too late to take it back, and by the flash in Finn's gaze, he knew he'd struck a nerve. "So you work for yourselves?"

"Yeah, pretty much. We have a manager, but he works for us, not the other way around."

Danny thought over the day he'd just spent with his DCI riding his arse for statistics that didn't exist. "I like the sound of that."

"It suits us." Finn paused like he was weighing his words. "It suits us artistically because we can play whatever we want, whenever we want—surfer festivals, hippie communes, whatever—but it's more than that. I've toured with big bands, and it sucks the life from you, you know? It's all about the money, and I hate that."

"Corporate machine, eh?"

"Exactly. I don't need a soulless record contract to validate me. Jack got dicked on by a record company a few years ago. They took advantage of him because he didn't know any better. I don't want any fucker to have that power over me."

Danny smiled. He couldn't help it. Angry Finn was a sight to fucking behold. "Jack's your drummer, right? And your housemate?"

"Yeah, when he's not in the studio or smashing the clubs." Finn relaxed, mollified by the change of subject. "He's not around much, though. He works away a lot, and his boyfriend lives in Leeds."

"Why don't they live together?"

Finn shrugged. "I've been asking that for years. I think Jack would like it, but his fella's got this thing in his head about Jack sowing his oats."

The waiter interrupted them with the pakoras Finn had ordered to keep them going. Danny waited for him to leave. "Sowing his oats? What the fuck does that mean?"

"Jack's only ever been with Will. I mean, he's been with birds and stuff, but Will's the only bloke."

"So?"

Finn stuffed half a pakora in his mouth. "I know, right? But I think Will's worried Jack hasn't… I don't know, explored his sexuality properly? They're best mates, you see. They grew up together, and I reckon Will doesn't want to be Jack's easy option."

"Sounds complicated." And alien. Danny didn't have any gay friends up north.

"It's them." Finn said. "I stay out of it."

"You and Jack are close, though?" Danny had seen the photos scattered around the house Finn and Jack shared. Both tall and shaggy haired, they looked like brothers.

"You ask a lot of questions."

Danny shrugged. "Sorry. Comes with the job."

"Makes sense." Finn leaned forward. "Like when you told me your job. I'd been trying to figure you out, then it all clicked into place."

"I'm a copper, not MI5, mate."

Finn sniggered. "I know, but you're still pretty mysterious. Until I found your number on the fridge, I thought I'd never see you again."

There wasn't much Danny could say to that. He'd woken alone in Finn's bed on Monday morning with the intention of calling a cab home and confining Finn to the back of his mind. A moment of madness had seen him slapping his contact card on Finn's fridge. A moment of madness he couldn't bring himself to regret. "I wasn't sure you'd want to. It's been a while since I—"

"Shagged someone more than once?"

Danny chuckled. "That obvious?"

"I know your type. You're either a manwhore, married, or in the closet." Finn sat back while the waiter cleared the table and set a heated plate stand down. When the waiter was gone, he leaned forward and put his elbows on the table. "You're too nice to be a slag and too good in bed to be married, so I'm figuring it's the closet. Am I right?"

Danny felt his stomach turn over, perturbed he'd been

read so easily. "You're a little right. I'm not in the closet, but I'm not out at work."

"And work comes first, so you live the rest of your life in secret."

It wasn't a question, and for the first time, the spark between them dimmed. Danny searched for the words to explain himself. "It's not as absolute as you make it sound. My sex life isn't relevant to my job."

"Since when was being gay all about sex?"

"It isn't, but coming out to my department is a ball ache I don't need."

The squeaky wheels of an old-fashioned waiter's trolley gave Danny a reprieve. Soon the table was piled high with more food than Danny remembered ordering.

When the waiter was gone, Finn nudged Danny's leg. "I'm not having a go—I just don't get it. Why do you coppers get such a hard time for being queer? I thought times had changed."

Danny shrugged. "What you read in the papers doesn't relate much to reality. Half the blokes on my squad still call me a chink. Fuck knows what they'd say if they knew I was gay."

"Does it matter? It's only words, right?"

Danny suppressed a sigh. Finn had been on his mind all week, and never once had he pictured himself trying to explain the archaic mind-set of the police force. "It would be more subtle than just calling me a poofter. Like not answering the phone when I need backup, not passing on information I need for my cases or following up leads when I'm not around. Sounds like bollocks, but I've seen it happen before, and I can't afford to let it happen to me. Not out there…." Danny trailed off as he realized he was about to say too much. What was it about this bloke that scrambled his verbal filter? "Anyway… yeah. It's complicated. Maybe in a few years, if I make DS or something. Are we going to eat this shit or what?"

Danny had eaten with Finn enough to know how much he liked his food, and for the brief moments it took to fill their plates, Danny figured he'd shut the door on the copper conversation.

"So you're on the vice squad? With all the hookers and shit?"

Or maybe not. Danny shoved a forkful of madras in his mouth and claimed a raggedy piece of naan before Finn ate it all. "Yeah. I started in London, then transferred up here eighteen months ago. But there's more to it than prostitution, like gambling, narcotics, weapons."

"Weapons? You mean, like, guns?"

Danny chuckled darkly. "Or machetes. We seized a house full of them this week."

Finn was quiet a moment. Danny took his chance and changed the subject. "What about you? What do you do when you're not playing? I can tell you're a northern git, but you're not a Nottingham lad, are you?"

"Nah, I grew up in Derby. My folks have a boarding kennel there."

"Is that in the city?"

"No, Matlock. I don't like big cities."

Again with the crowds. Danny wondered if Finn's dislike of the outside world had anything to do with his band's decision to contain their success. "Dogs or cats?"

"Hmm?" Finn looked up from his plate.

"The kennel. Dogs or cats?"

"Both. My mum's a cat person. My old man likes the dogs."

"What about you?"

Finn sat back and rubbed his belly. Despite the mountain of food they'd started with, they'd put a substantial hole in it already. "Dunno. I spent most of my childhood cleaning up after the bloody things, so I'm pretty... what's that word?"

"Ambivalent?"

"That'll do. Yeah, I like them both, but I'd rather have a cat these days. Less work."

Danny snorted. "Tell that to my dad. My mum has four house cats. They fucking stink."

"Are you close to her?"

"My mum? God no." Danny pushed his plate away. "She's... difficult to be around. She has strange ideas and expectations. I can't win with her, so I've stopped trying."

"Because you're gay?"

"That doesn't help, but it's not even that interesting. I'm just not who she thought I would be. Maybe she'll have better luck with my sister."

Finn winced. The waiter cleared their plates and brought a tray of fennel seeds and jelly beans. They picked at it until Danny realized it was two o'clock in the morning and he was due on shift at dawn.

They fought over the bill. Finn won and paid before Danny could stop him. "Sneaky git. My turn next time."

Finn threw a grin over his shoulder as Danny followed him out of the restaurant. "Next time? Haven't scared you off, then?"

They stepped out into the frigid night air. Danny blew on his hands. "Scared me with what? Scarfing all my rice?"

Finn grinned and started walking in the direction of Danny's car. Danny followed on autopilot, though he'd neglected to ask how Finn was getting home. Something clicked in his brain when Finn stopped by the VW van he'd passed earlier.

"*...good to see Finn smiling again, ain't it? It's been too long, man....*"

Interesting. For Danny, Finn's smile was all he could see.

Finn leaned on the van. "This is me."

"Um." Danny faltered. He didn't know what to say. They'd spent much of the night leaning over the table, heads together, legs unobtrusively entwined, but what next? They already shagged the shit out of each other. Why was a good-night kiss so fucking terrifying?

Finn caught Danny's sleeve, tugged him closer. "Can I really see you again?"

"Said so, didn't I?"

Danny placed his palms either side of Finn's head and glanced around, all the while feeling the silent siren call of being so close to Finn. He scanned the dark streets. They were in a dubious part of the city, but he couldn't see anyone lurking. And part of him didn't care, a part that grew louder and stronger with every inch Finn leaned forward. Their lips met in a kiss that brought their stolen weekend together rushing back and lit a fuse Danny couldn't contain. He pushed Finn against the van, pressed into him, absorbed him, lost himself in all that was Finn—scruff, clean sweat, and man. Let Finn pull his hair and squeeze bruises onto his hips.

Then Finn pulled away, breathless, his gaze clouded by something Danny didn't understand. "If we're going to do this again, there's something I have to tell you."

CHAPTER FIVE

FINN TOOK a deep breath and pulled away with all the conviction he could muster.

Danny's crooked smile faded. "Is this the bit when you tell me you just want to be mates?"

"I hope not." Finn forced a grin. It felt off, and by the uncertainty creeping into Danny's gaze, Finn reckoned he thought so too.

Finn stepped away. Reconnecting with Danny tonight had made him feel lighter than air, but the weight of his confession had brought him back to earth with a bump. He was already more attached to Danny than he cared to admit, but he hadn't envisioned them having this conversation so soon, perhaps not even at all. Danny didn't seem the type to stick around, even without the bullshit Finn had to tell him.

So don't tell him....

Finn swallowed temptation. Lying—by omission, if nothing else—wasn't an option. He'd been down that road before, and it never led anywhere nice. Besides, he'd given up on shame a long time ago.... Most days, at least.

"Finn?"

Shit. Finn felt his stress levels rise, and with it his mind slowed and blurred, making it hard to organize his thoughts. He took Danny's arm and pointed to the curb. "Let's sit."

"Here?" Danny glanced around uneasily but followed Finn's lead and dropped down beside him. "You're freaking me out now. Can't be that bad, whatever it is."

"Depends on your interpretation of bad."

"Try me."

Finn met Danny's gaze. Under the cloud of the frosty night, his eyes looked liquid and deep, like Finn could dive into them and never reach the bottom. Could he trust eyes like that? Could he trust Danny?

He didn't know the answer to either question, but it didn't matter. Trust or not, the alternative was pulling away before Danny worked things out for himself, and he couldn't bear that. The idiot in him wanted to hope for the best.

Here goes nothing….

"I'm schizophrenic."

Silence.

Danny blinked. "What?"

"I have schizophrenia." Finn fought the urge to look down and hide from whatever reaction was coming. He'd seen them all over the years—horror, disgust, derision… fear— why was this any different? Why was *Danny* any different?

Finn couldn't tell because for a long moment, Danny said nothing, face blank, gaze inscrutable. Finn wished he had a cigarette, but he'd quit years ago. "Don't worry. I'm not going to stab you or anything."

Danny looked startled. "Why would I be worried about that?"

Finn shrugged. "That's what everyone thinks, isn't it? That we're all psychotic old-lady killers."

"I don't think that," Danny said. "And trust me, I've met plenty of nonschizophrenics who did want to stab me."

That gave Finn pause for thought. Danny didn't seem to like talking about his job, and Finn wondered if there was more to it than simply Danny not being out. Hookers, drugs, weapons. None of it sounded pleasant.

"How bad is it?" Danny picked at something on his jeans. He hadn't moved away yet, but Finn felt the new distance between them. It hurt, and he braced himself for it to get worse.

"I'm on the mild end of the spectrum," Finn said. "It's managed well, but I've spent time in hospital with it in the past, especially in the beginning."

"How long have you had it?"

Again with the questions. Finn forced himself to look at Danny. "I've always been a bit nutty, and they reckon my genes predisposed me to it, but the schizophrenia was triggered by a bad trip when I was nineteen. Sent me totally round the bend. Took ages to come back."

"An acid trip?"

"Yeah." Finn hugged his knees to his chest. "I was on tour with a band who thought they were Pink Floyd. I'd done acid and shrooms before, but I guess this was just one trip too far."

More silence. Finn wondered if Danny had already checked out, but then he felt a hand on his back, cautious and light but undeniable.

"You're twenty-seven, right? So you've had it… eight years?" Danny appeared lost in thought, but Finn could see his mind whirring. "What's the reality? Day to day, I mean. Do you have help?"

Finn bristled. Help? Why did everyone assume he was a fucking basket case? "I get by. I've got good mates who understand it's not some modern-day bloody leprosy."

Danny sensed Finn's tone and finally met his gaze, though he couldn't quite hide his surprise. "People know?"

"Some. It's not something I hide, but there are plenty of people in my life who have no idea."

"Is this why you don't drink?"

Questions, questions, questions. Danny's reaction hadn't been what Finn had feared, but for some reason, despite

Danny's hand on his back, the cold, clinical inquisition felt worse.

Finn's patience snapped. He stood. Danny looked startled but remained on the ground, watching, analyzing, perhaps deciding if Finn was worth the hassle. Fuck that. Finn had come out the wrong side of that debate before, and he wasn't going to let someone else turn their back on him. "Look, it is what it is. This is me, but I don't expect you to live with it. You wouldn't be the first bloke to run for the hills, so don't fucking worry about it, okay?"

He got in the van without waiting for Danny's response, and he drove away, half an eye on Danny still sitting on the pavement and his heart sinking into his stomach. He hated this part. No matter how many times his condition pushed people away, it never got any easier.

Maybe you should get that bloody cat and be done with it.

"You don't have to do this, you know." Finn kept his gaze on the busy Nottingham traffic. "I've been by myself before. Loads of times."

Jack's boyfriend, Will, looked up from his phone and grinned the shy, boyish grin that made him so endearing. "Don't give me that shit. I know Jack usually drives you home after. Do you think we don't talk?"

Finn shrugged 'cause that was a question he didn't want to answer. Jack was a good mate, but he and Will were a funny couple—totally in love, but without direction… a bigger picture. Finn always got the impression they were waiting for life to guide them, show them what they should be doing. Fuck that. Life was for living, not waiting.

Yeah, that's why you're waiting on a call that's never bloody coming.

"Anyway," Will said. "Jack was supposed to come home today, but his flight got delayed, so I could use the company."

Finn snorted. "I'm not great company after a day in the loony bin, but have at it."

Will said nothing and Finn left him alone. Truth be told, he *did* like someone with him after he'd had his monthly injection. He didn't get many side effects these days—he'd been on the same drug long enough—but the twenty-four hours of… nothing… the numbness sometimes unnerved him.

He swung the van into the clinic car park. He was early, a habit leftover from darker days when he'd struggled to organize his time, but the nurses were used to him here. Got him in and out quickly so he could go home and wait for his soul to come back.

"Do you want me to come in with you?"

Finn jumped out of the van and glanced over his shoulder. The waiting room of the clinic often freaked him out, but did he want Will to see him have antipsychotics pumped into his arsecheek? Probably not. "You can wait with me if you like, but you don't have to come *in* in."

"Lead the way."

Finn sighed and did just that. He left Will next to a particularly chatty fellow patient and went to the desk to sign himself in. When he came back, he caught the woman's musical accent. Welsh. He'd seen the woman many times before, but he'd never noticed it before. He sat back in his seat and thought of the faint melodic warmth in Danny's voice, a lilt that seemed out of place with his Asian complexion. Welsh-Chinese. Who knew it was such a killer combination?

Finn pondered the theory while he fleshed out a tune he'd had on his mind since he'd first spotted Danny sitting alone at the bar after that gig. From a distance, Danny had looked like he had the weight of the world on his shoulders, and the lonely, mournful melody had seemed to fit. He'd doubted himself when he'd claimed his place by Danny's side and bought him a few drinks. Danny had laughed a lot, but after their fateful curry date, the scratched-out song had come back to Finn. He traced the chord pattern with his fingers, tapped out a rhythm with his foot—

Will kicked him. "Fuck's sake. You're as bad as Jack. Why can't you musicians ever sit still?"

Finn rolled his eyes, but a nurse called his name before he could retaliate.

"Mr. McGovern?"

Finn rose and followed the nurse into the doctor's office. She left him with the obligatory questionnaire. He filled it out, restraining himself from being sarcastic and reminding himself to update his self-care plan. Jack had been his crutch for a while now. Poor bloke probably needed a break.

Ten minutes later Finn left the clinic with his blood loaded with the drugs that kept him sane.

"That was quick," Will remarked. "Want me to drive home?"

Finn considered the question. Some days he felt fine after his depot injection, but today he could already feel the drug seeping into him, calming the monster within and leaving the rest of him next to useless. "Yeah, mate. Could you?"

"No problem."

The journey home passed in a haze. Finn grew more detached with each mile, and by the time Will parked outside the house, he felt like the walking dead.

He slid out of the van with weighted legs and followed Will into the house. He considered going straight to bed, but Will guided him to the couch and disappeared to put the kettle on. Alone in the living room, Finn set his phone carefully on the coffee table and lay back. He could already feel his mind slowing, shutting down, and knew it wouldn't be long before the blank oblivion took over. He stared hard at his phone, willing it to ring, knowing that somewhere beneath it all, he desperately wanted it to, but nothing happened and he was asleep before Will came back with the tea.

Will woke Finn that evening with the lure of a Chinese take-away and a *Dad's Army* boxed set. "What do you want to eat? Chow mein or chop suey?"

Finn sat up and rubbed his heavy eyes. Chop suey. Why did that ring a bell? He thought about it, but nothing came back to him. "What are you having?"

"Ribs and sweet-and-sour pork balls."

"You know Chinese people don't eat that shit, don't you?" Finn's gaze fell on his still silent phone. He remembered Danny, but as he'd feared, he felt nothing. "They make that fluorescent pink stuff just for us."

"I don't care who else eats it. I'm fucking starving."

Finn glanced at the window and saw the day had faded to a dark winter night while he'd been sleeping. He checked the time: 8:00 p.m. Oops. That was four hours of his life he'd never get back. "You didn't have to wait for me, mate. I probably won't eat it anyway."

"You might change your mind when it gets here."

Finn grunted. Left to his own devices, he'd probably stare at a blank TV until the blast of drugs wore off.

Will came back with his laptop, and despite a tranquilizer-induced haze of apathy, Finn leaned forward and took a look at Will's work-in-progress designs for the Lamps' website.

"Nice." Finn wasn't much for branding, but he had to admit Will had a touch that obscured the corporate commercialism Finn hated so much. And he didn't take himself too seriously… the bastard. Finn pointed at the screen. "You made my graphic a bloody koala?"

Will laughed and dodged Finn's halfhearted punch. "Don't blame me. When you guys said you didn't want to use photos of yourselves, I was going to use manga characters. It was you who suggested animals."

Finn tried to scowl. It didn't work. His face felt numb. "You could've made me a wolf or something. How come Jack gets to be a gorilla?"

"He's not a gorilla, he's a chimp, and trust me, it bloody

suits him." Will beckoned Finn closer to the screen. "Here, look… we can make you cool. What kind of guitar do you want? Acoustic or electric?"

Finn watched Will work his magic, adding a guitar, a harmonica, and a weird fedora-style hat human Finn wouldn't be caught dead in. "Still think you're taking the bloody piss. Fucking koala."

Will pressed a few more buttons, then closed his laptop. "If you really hate it, I can change it, but you should totally blame Jack. I asked him to describe you in two words, and he said shy and cuddly."

"How the hell would he know I'm cuddly? I've never cuddled that bloke in my life."

"Not denying it, though, are you? And you're lying. I've seen the photos from Download last year." Will reached for his phone, no doubt to text Jack and tell him his joke had gone down like a lead balloon.

Finn lay back on the couch. The brief interaction with Will had exhausted him, and he got the feeling Will had been tasked with keeping him awake until he'd eaten his supper, a theory proved when Will nudged him out of a fast-approaching doze.

"Jack said you've been seeing someone. Who is it? Anyone I know?"

That woke Finn up. Since his ill-fated conversation with Danny, he'd stopped talking to Jack about him. He couldn't face admitting his condition had sent yet another bloke running in the opposite direction, and there was little he could say about Danny without betraying his trust. Danny hadn't outright asked Finn not to tell anyone he was a copper, but he didn't have to. Finn *knew*. "I don't think I'm seeing him anymore. I told him I was a nutjob."

Will winced and his grin faded. "What did he say?"

"Nothing, and he hasn't called since."

"That's a shitter. You need someone to keep you company in this big old house when Jack's away."

45

"Thought you were my new babysitter?"

"Don't be a bellend—"

The doorbell rang. Will started to get up, but Finn stilled him. "I'll go, and I'm paying. You've done enough for me today."

Finn heaved himself from the sofa and shuffled to the front door, counting cash carefully out of his wallet, his brain like mud. He opened the door with his gaze down, focused.

A warm, familiar hand on his arm felt like a bloody Taser.

CHAPTER SIX

FINN BLINKED slowly. "It's you."

"The very same." Danny chanced a grin. "Your phone was off and I was in the area, so I figured...."

"Right."

Danny opened his mouth. Shut it again. He wasn't entirely sure how he'd ended up on Finn's doorstep, and Finn's nonplussed frown wasn't helping. "Are you all right?"

"What?" Finn looked blankly between Danny and his open wallet. "Yeah. Sorry. I thought you were someone else."

"Finn?" A new voice came from somewhere in the house.

Finn turned and Danny saw another blond bloke behind him, a bloke who wasn't Finn's housemate. Danny's heart sank. Was he too late already?

The blond guy came up beside Finn and took his wallet. For the first time, Danny noticed yet another bloke was behind *him* holding a flimsy white takeaway bag. Shit. How long had he been there?

Finn seemed taken aback too. "Uh, this is Will, Jack's boyfriend."

That made sense, though the way Finn was looking through him felt a little odd—so odd Danny wasn't convinced Finn was even talking to him.

Who else would he be talking to?

Danny killed the thought before it manifested in his brain. Over the past week he'd convinced himself Finn's illness didn't worry him. Stopped himself from rehashing their short time together, searching for clues there was something fundamentally wrong with Finn.

Wrong. Danny scratched that word out too. It didn't fit Finn. None of it did—not the disquiet Danny had felt when he'd first heard the word schizophrenia, nor the hours and hours of Internet research he'd done since. Hypnotic voice and enchanting smile aside, Finn just seemed so… normal.

Will sidestepped Danny and paid the deliveryman. He nudged Finn. "Are you inviting your mate in or what?"

"This is Danny," Finn said to no one in particular, and then he seemed to refocus. He stared hard at Danny's hand, which was still on his arm, then took it and tugged. "Come in."

Will shut the door behind them. He cast a keen gaze over Finn, then pulled a couple of containers from the takeaway bag and handed the bag to Finn. "Take this in the living room, mate."

Finn disappeared without a backward glance. Danny thought about following him, but a hard look from Will stayed him. He was a scrawny fella, but Danny could tell he had something to say.

"Are you the bloke Finn's been seeing?"

Danny shrugged. "Unless he's been seeing anyone else."

"Finn's not like that." Will shifted his takeaway containers to his other hand. "And you know, right? It was you he told?"

Ah. Danny finally caught on. "Yeah. He told me last week. Is he okay? He seems a little…."

"He had his depot injection today, so he's a bit spaced." Will put one foot on the stairs. "I'm going upstairs, but make sure he eats something, okay? Oh, and if you leave, come and get me."

Depot injection. Danny had read about those, holed up in

his car in the red-light district, but Lexi had turned up on her corner before he'd gleaned much knowledge, and Will disappeared before he could pick his brain.

Danny drifted to the living room and found Finn staring at the TV. "*Dad's Army*?"

"Better than bloody *Red Dwarf*." Finn stared at Danny with his strangely dead eyes. "I know I'm pleased to see you, but I'm not feeling it."

"I can go if you want?"

Finn shook his head. "That's not what I mean. Sit down, please?"

Danny shed his coat, draped it over the arm of the couch, and sat bedside Finn, close enough to feel his body heat. "How often do you have these injections?"

If Finn was surprised Danny knew the source of his odd behavior, he didn't show it. "Every month. They keep me sane, but the jabs knock me out for a little while."

"I was worried when you turned your phone off." Worried was an understatement. It had taken him a few days to find the balls to pick up the phone, and the dead line had scared the shit out of him.

Finn retrieved his phone from the coffee table. He pressed the screen. Nothing happened. "Shit. It must've died on me. When did you call?"

"This morning."

"What were you going to say?"

"Hmm?"

"When you called."

Danny considered that. There was no denying Finn's condition had shocked him… thrown him, but despite Finn's flat apathy now, Danny wasn't ready to give up on them. "I was going to ask you out."

"Yeah? Where were we gonna go?"

"Assuming you said yes, I was gonna take you to Batman's house."

Finn's expression turned wistful. "Wollaton Hall? Then I definitely would've said yes. I love that place."

"That the only reason?"

"That I'd say yes? No… I don't think so."

That was good enough for now. Danny's gaze fell on the abandoned bag of food, and he remembered Will's instructions. "What have you got in there?"

Finn thought a moment. "Chinese, maybe? Where did Will go? He knows."

"Upstairs." Danny snagged the bag. "Do you want me to get him?"

Finn scowled. "He got to you, didn't he? Told you how *fragile* I am."

"No, he just said you need to eat your dinner."

Finn's irritation almost made Danny snigger, but he caught it in time. He pulled containers out of the bag and set them on the coffee table. "Chow mein and… hang on, something pink. Sweet and sour, maybe?"

A flicker of amusement brightened Finn's face. Encouraged, Danny got up and went to the kitchen for cutlery, paper towels, and a bottle of water. As he shut the fridge, he saw his number still stuck to the door. The sight of it made him smile, though he still wasn't quite sure what had possessed him to leave it there.

Finn was upright when Danny got back, though he'd made no move to open the containers of food.

Danny filled a plate, sat close to Finn, and handed him a fork. "Eat. Then I'll leave you alone, I promise."

"I don't want you to leave me alone."

Finn turned his attention to picking at his food without elaborating. Danny did the same and watched Finn in his peripheral vision, slightly perturbed. He'd grown used to the way Finn usually inhaled his food.

When they were done eating, Danny cleared up. He came back to a sleepy-looking Finn and wondered if he should go, but somehow even with his eyes half closed, Finn sensed his indecision.

"Don't go. We need to talk about this."

Danny leaned on the doorframe. "It can wait until you're feeling better."

Finn lifted his head from the back of the sofa. "I don't feel bad, Danny. I don't feel anything."

Danny didn't get it. He tried to imagine life without the roiling buzz that came from a cracked case or the simmering heat that came from simply being near Finn. Couldn't do it. "Do you *want* to talk about it?"

"It's not going anywhere," Finn said. "Might as well get it all out in the open, so you can figure out what you want."

"What I want? What about you?"

Finn shrugged. "Nothing changes for me. It is what it is. But you... you've had a week to think on it and here you are, so I'm guessing you have some questions?"

It is what it is.

Finn had used that phrase before, and it made Danny's chest ache, though he couldn't say why. He reclaimed his place on the couch. Truth be told he did have questions, bloody loads of them, but he'd pushed Finn too far before—hurt him—and he couldn't bear to do that again. "I don't want to dig out your soul, mate. You know what this means better than I do. What do I need to know?"

"Now there's a question." Finn blew out a breath. "Sometimes it's hard to tell what's a symptom and what's just me."

He stopped. Danny nudged him. "Like what?"

"Like my inability to organize my time and the fixation on music. Sometimes I watch Jack spend all weekend obsessing over a bass line and figure it comes with the territory, but then he goes away or something else happens, and I'm back to thinking I'm a freak."

"You're not a freak."

Finn laughed, dark and flat, not like Finn at all. "Yeah,

right," Finn said. "You want to know if I hear voices, don't you? If I talk to myself and see things that aren't there?"

Danny held his tongue, but Finn either knew him too well already or he'd had this conversation more times than he cared to remember.

"Not often, is the answer." Finn sat back and put his feet up on the coffee table. "The injections work for me, and even when I think I am slipping, it's usually me overthinking something."

"Overthinking?"

"Yeah. I imagine my imagination. Lucky me, eh?"

Danny tried to make sense of that sentence. Nope. Not happening. "You've lost me."

Finn shrugged. "The everyday bollocks bothers me more than the episodes. They're pretty sporadic these days. I spend more time worrying about relapsing than actually doing it."

"When was your last, er, episode?"

Finn shot Danny a hard look. "I haven't had a serious one in years, but I can be a bit slow. If something isn't instinctive for me, it takes me a while to figure it out. I get agitated some-times too, if I'm stressed or tired or working too much, which is fucking annoying."

"How so?"

"My music is my life, you know? It calms me, distracts me. It's my safe place. I lose my shit when it goes wrong. That's when you'll find me hiding in the cellar."

Danny leaned back and mirrored Finn's pose. Finn shifted a little closer. Another inch and they'd be touching, but they weren't done yet. "What happens when you're ill? Who looks after you?"

"Depends how bad it is…. Jack, mainly. He's a good mate. Sometimes I go home to my mum, but she gets upset if it goes on too long. I have a self-care plan and advance statements in case things get bad. If you're still around in a few months, I'll show them to you."

"So you want me to stick around, then?"

"If you want."

It wasn't a question, or perhaps it was. Danny's mind raced so much he couldn't tell. In any case, Finn's bone-weary yawn told Danny he'd had enough questions for one day. Finn tipped his head back, eyes closed, breathing deep and even. Danny watched him fall asleep and pondered how strange it was that Finn looked more alive in that moment than he had all night.

"DIRTY PIG cunt. Ain't you got nothing better to do?"

Danny rolled his eyes and shut the car door on his mouthy suspect. The bloke was wanted in connection with supplying GHB to schoolboys. Danny had been on his tail for months, and his persistence had paid off. Endless nights loitering outside youth clubs and crappy pubs known for serving underage teens had finally come to fruition. Shame it came with three hours of paperwork.

The panda car drove off into the night. Danny drifted back to his unmarked car, flipping idly through the notes he'd need when he got back to the station to interview the suspect. He was looking forward to it. The bloke's crime was pretty fucking sinister, but in truth he was doing a village out of a good idiot. Only luck had kept him on the street so long.

Danny drove back to the station and retrieved his perp. His phone beeped in his pocket as they waited their turn with the desk sergeant. He ignored it, knowing it was Finn, but he couldn't ignore the flutter in his chest. He and Finn had been texting nonstop since Danny had spent an uncomfortable night on Finn's couch, watching Finn sleep, squeezing his hand, tracing the ink on his fingers….

Fuck's sake.

Danny gave himself an internal shake. Finn had still been out of it the following morning. Danny hadn't had time to go back, and it was hard to tell over text if Finn was back to his normal self, or at least what Danny perceived as normal. Despite their run of heavy conversations, in reality they still hardly new each other.

Didn't stop him grinning like a bloody idiot every time Finn's name flashed up on the screen.

It was four hours later, and eight o'clock in the morning, before Danny read the message.

Enough small talk. I want to see you again… soon.

Danny debated calling Finn straight back, but he knew from their lighter conversations that Finn wasn't an early riser. Instead he drove home, took a much-needed shower, and decamped to the sofa with tea and toast to wait for the clock to tick by to a more godly hour.

Finn's call woke him sometime later. Danny fumbled for his phone and squinted at the screen. His head ached and his eyes felt scratchy and raw from his overnight shift, but Finn's grinning Facebook photo brought Danny awake in a hazy rush of anticipation. "Hey, stranger."

Finn chuckled. "Hope you don't mean that literally."

"Not at all." Danny stretched the kinks out of his neck. "How's tricks?"

Danny threw out the casual question with little thought, absent and automatic. He expected Finn's answer to be in the same vein, so he was surprised when Finn cut to the chase.

"Better. Listen, I'm sorry you had to see that…. Shit, actually, I'm not sorry. It's my reality and I'm not ashamed of it, but if I'd had my way, you wouldn't have seen it so soon."

Danny blinked a few times and focused on the clock at the bottom of the news channel. Damn. This was a heavy conversation for 10:00 a.m. "I didn't mind."

"I did…. At least I do now. Didn't mind much at the time. Can't remember most of it."

"No?" Danny switched the TV off. "Probably not much to remember, then."

Finn snorted, but it sounded resigned. "You don't have to pretend, you know."

"Pretend what?"

"That it didn't happen… that I wasn't bumbling around like a fucking basket case. I know what I'm like when I've had that jab. I got Jack to video me once."

"Really? Why did you do that?"

"I was curious," Finn said. "And scared. I don't like gaps in my head. I felt better when I'd seen why they were there with my own eyes."

Finn's candor made Danny's chest ache. Finn was so brave and matter-of-fact in the face of a condition that must be terrifying. "There wasn't much to see the other night. We talked, ate, and fell asleep."

"Nice try." Finn sounded amused, but when he spoke again, Danny felt the air shift. "You don't have to do this, Danny. I'm a big boy, and I can take it if you don't want to deal with my bullshit."

"It's not bullshit."

"I know, I'm just crap with words. Whatever—just hear me out. Being a schizophrenic is a bloody ball ache, and I wouldn't blame you if you walked away. If it's too much, we need to knock this shit on the head now… right now. I can't—"

"Can't what?" Danny pressed gently.

Finn sighed. "Never mind. Just think about it, okay? I'm not the easiest bloke to be with sometimes."

"Neither am I." Danny got up and walked to the window. "I work long hours—day and night—and my last boyfriend said I was an emotional cripple."

"Yeah? When did he say that?"

Danny counted back in time. "Six years ago, maybe? It's been so long I can't remember."

Finn was silent a moment. Danny wondered what he was thinking, wondered if perhaps his get-out clause for Danny was a double bluff. Maybe *Finn* was the one who wanted to bail.

Danny stared at his reflection in the window. Two days of

stubble. Hair on end. He looked like hell and suddenly felt reckless. It was time to put his cards on the table. "Listen, mate. The schizophrenia doesn't bother me. At least not the way you think it does. It doesn't put me off, it just makes me… I don't know. Worry about you, I guess, for your sake, not mine."

"You don't need to worry about me, Danny. I'm just fine. Better than that, I'm happy."

"Happy, eh? Works for me. I'll be happy if you'll be happy."

"Yeah?" Danny heard the smile in Finn's voice. "That sounds like a plan."

A plan sounded like progress, but Danny figured asking Finn to elaborate would make him sound like a knobhead. Instead he said nothing and hoped for the best, a practice that rarely turned out well for him. But for someone who thought they were crap with words, Finn had a way of bringing a conversation full circle.

"Good," Finn said. "If you can handle my questionable sanity, I can deal with you being an emo retard."

"I'm not a bloody emo."

Finn chuckled. "Whatever. I'm playing a solo gig tonight over in Mansfield. Come down if you're not busy. We can do something after."

DANNY DIDN'T take much persuading. After snatching another few hours of well-earned sleep and making a half-arsed effort to clean his flat, he took a shower and drove west out of the city.

Mansfield wasn't an area Danny knew well. He parked his car outside the dubious pub Finn had directed him to. What was it with this bloke and dumps like these? Inside, though, the pub wasn't as bad as Danny had feared. In fact with the roaring log fire and scent of mulled cider, it was more than decent.

Danny shut the door on the frosty night and headed for the bar. He bought a mug of hot cider and scanned the crowded pub. The textured, honeyed tones of Finn's voice reeled him in like a siren call, but it took Danny a moment to spot his shaggy blond hair on a small stage in the pub's cozy alcove.

Yep. Still gorgeous.

Danny felt a familiar warmth creep through him. He found a seat at the bar and soaked up the easy atmosphere of the pub. It was a far cry from the Lamps' rowdy gig, but isolated and alone on stage, just a mic and his guitar, the laid-back vibe fit Finn like a glove. Danny relaxed. He'd loved the Lamps' gig, but this felt more intimate, and it suited his mood.

Finn strummed his way through an eclectic set list, mixing up crowd-pleasers with unfamiliar songs Danny assumed were his own work. Danny loved it all, even discounting his unhealthy fixation with Finn's hair. The gig passed in a flash, and Finn's call for last-minute requests caught him off guard.

Danny bit his tongue. There were so many songs he'd love to hear Finn sing, but he wasn't sure Finn had seen him come in, and announcing his presence in front of a crowd of ale-swilling locals felt all wrong.

Besides, Finn's audience seemed to know him and had plenty requests of their own. It wasn't until the third song that Danny knew for sure Finn had spotted him lurking at the back. He heard the waver in his voice and saw the flash of heat in his hazel eyes—a heat that matched the stirring in Danny's heart.

Finn strummed the last few chords of his own unique take of "Supersonic." He smiled, and though he didn't meet Danny's gaze, Danny knew the smile was for him. "Last one, folks. Give me something good."

An elderly man called out a song. Finn chuckled. "Not my usual remit, but I'll give it a go."

He picked out a melody. Tapped out a rhythm on the back of his guitar. The chord pattern that followed was unfamiliar, but Danny recognized the lyrics. Fats Domino. "Ain't That a Shame." Danny's father had played it every Sunday when they'd lived in the old house in Swansea, but he hadn't heard it in years, and Finn's grungy twist on the old jazz classic was something else.

The gig wrapped up. Finn set his guitar down and Danny found himself out of his seat and pushing through the crowd before he knew what he was doing. He reached the front as Finn stepped offstage and was rewarded with the brightest grin he'd ever seen. The connection was instant. Finn stepped right into Danny's personal space, and Danny stared, transfixed. Gone were the dead, shadowed eyes of just a few days before. Finn was back and more beautiful than ever.

Danny swallowed hard, mindful of the people around them. He hadn't spotted anyone who looked like a copper, but why would he? His squad was small, and they kept to themselves as much as possible. There were few beat coppers Danny would recognize out of uniform.

Maybe sensing Danny's dilemma, or perhaps wanting to avoid the crowd for his own reasons, Finn grabbed Danny's arm and yanked him into a deserted back room. Danny went willingly and spun them around, pressing Finn back against the closed door. "All right, mate?"

"I am now. Wasn't sure you'd come."

"I was." Danny tucked a stray lock of Finn's shaggy hair behind his ear, then put his palms flat on the grimy door. "Good gig?"

Finn shrugged, a tiny frown creasing his forehead. "Yeah, I guess. I play here a lot. I like the vibe. Wasn't sure you would, though. Thought it might be too boring for you."

"You're joking, right? I love this shit. I'd watch someone play in their nan's living room if they were any good."

Finn smiled and leaned forward, his face inches from Danny's. He took a breath, but instead of words came a kiss that made Danny sway on his feet.

Danny forgot himself. He pushed Finn back against the door and kissed the shit out of him. Absorbed him. Touched his heated skin and scratched the rough scruff on his jaw. Finn moaned and dug his nails into Danny's chest. The touch lit Danny on fire. He pulled away. Snogging in the backroom of a workingmen's pub was a bad idea at the best of times. They needed to leave. Now. "Are you done for the night?"

"Ten minutes." Finn let his hands drop. "I need to pack up my gear. Meet you at the bar?"

Danny tilted his head, listening to the hum of the crowded pub. The place was packed shoulder to shoulder. "Sure? I can wait here? Give you a hand?"

"Don't indulge the monster in my brain." Finn tapped his temple. "I'll find you."

Danny left him to it. Finn didn't seem the type to like being coddled, and though Danny felt relatively comfortable with Finn's condition, he still didn't know what the fuck to say when Finn said shit like that.

He made his way back to the bar. Finn's kiss had turned him inside out and he felt like a pint, but the hot cider in his belly and his car parked outside put paid to that. Instead he loitered close to the fire, people watching and eavesdropping on the rave reviews of Finn's set. Despite the bleak exterior, the pub was warm and welcoming, and Danny felt half-asleep when his phone rang in his pocket.

He pulled it out with a mind to rejecting the call and turning his phone off. The number on the screen stopped him. The DCI. Shit. His calls were never good news.

Danny answered the call and stepped outside. "Guv?"

"Evening, Danny. Sorry to bother you on your night off. Where are you at? Can you talk?"

"I'm out, but I'm good. What's up?"

"We've got a body out by the A52. IC1 female, early twenties. Uniform reckons it could be a tom."

Danny glanced over his shoulder, but no one had followed him out of the pub. "What makes them think it's a tom?"

"Track marks. Clothes. No ID. They're bringing her into Queen's. I want you to get over there and take a look. See if it's anyone you recognize."

"What's the COD?"

"Too early to tell, but they reckon she hasn't been out there for long. Hopefully it's just an OD, but we need to be sure. I don't want to be caught on the hop with this."

Danny scowled, glad his boss couldn't see him. *Just an OD.* Who cared if the dead bag of bones was someone's daughter or sister, right? Fuck's sake. The DCI was a good bloke, as bosses went, but bullshit like that wound Danny up. "I'm in Mansfield right now. I can be there in an hour. Are you sending anyone else?"

"Not yet." The DCI cleared his throat. "It might be nothing. Have a look. See what you think. Any questions?"

"Nope."

"Good. Update me in the morning, and keep it quiet, even in the office. If there's a connection with Manchester, we don't want it getting out unhandled."

"Guv."

Danny killed the call. It was too early to draw comparisons with the run of missing prostitutes in Manchester, but he kept his opinions to himself. The evidence, or lack of it, would do the talking.

He pocketed the phone. His mind was already slipping into work mode, but he needed to find Finn before he dashed across the city to examine a dead body.

He went back inside and found Finn shouldering his way through the crowd, the only sign of his discomfort the tight grins he sent the way of folk who called his name.

Danny met him halfway, curving himself around Finn in a

way that shielded most of him from the jostling crowd. "I gotta go. Work."

Finn's smile faded. "Work?"

"Yeah. My DCI called me in."

Finn was bumped from behind. He flinched and took a deep breath. Danny took his arm and pulled him as close as he dared in the crowded bar. "Do you need a lift home?"

"What?"

Danny leaned closer and repeated the question.

Finn shook his head. "Nah. The van's out the back."

Danny looked beyond Finn to the door he could hardly see through the throngs of people blocking their way. He needed to get a bloody shift on, but something, *everything* screamed at him not to leave until he'd seen Finn safely on his way home.

He put his mouth close to Finn's ear again, too close, but he was past caring. "Come on. I'll walk you out."

CHAPTER SEVEN

FINN PICKED out a melancholy melody on the battered ukulele he'd had since childhood. The wood was faded and chipped and covered with dubious stickers he'd never get off, but aside from his beloved Gibson, the tiny instrument was his favorite piece of kit.

He scribbled a chord sequence in his notebook. Bigsy, his main songwriting partner in the band, looked over his shoulder. "That's pretty blue. Thought we were working on a banger?"

Finn shrugged. Bigsy was a great bloke to write with, good at keeping Finn on track when he got distracted, but it wasn't working today. Finn was pissed off and lonely, and it was starting to show.

Lonely. Fuck's sake. Get a grip, man. Finn gave himself an internal shake. It had been a week since Danny had bailed on him, and they'd hardly spoken since, but they'd known each other less than a month. What the fuck did Finn think he was missing?

He went back to searching out the roof-lifting chorus he needed for Bigsy's stomping bass riff, but it was no good. His heart wasn't in it.

Bigsy sighed, his frustration clear. He was used to Finn's eccentric ways, but this kind of thing drove him nuts. Bigsy was a man who got things done. "All right, mate. Out with it."

"Hmm?"

Bigsy kicked Finn's shin. "Something's got your bottom lip stuck out so far yer gonna trip over it. What's up?"

Busted. Bigsy was the oldest member of the band by fifteen years, and he did his best to avoid the inevitable father-figure dynamic that created, but he was a shrewd bloke, and now he'd asked, Finn knew he wouldn't quit.

"I'm waiting for someone to call me."

"That bloke you've been seeing?"

"How do you know about that?"

Bigsy rolled his eyes. "No secrets in the band, Finn. You know that. Worse than a bunch of schoolgirls."

He had a point, but since Finn had discovered Danny wasn't out at work, he'd tried not to mention him to anyone but Jack and Will.

"So, what's the deal?" Bigsy said. "You split up?"

Finn shrugged. Danny had cried off from their casual date, blaming work, but the paranoid monster in Finn's mind kept telling him it was probably something else. "We're not together. I've only seen him a few times."

"Why the long face, then?"

Finn shrugged again. Danny had been nothing but sweet since the night he'd spent on Finn's sofa, watching Finn sleep through a drug coma, but the silence of the past few days stung. Finn had grown *way* too used to the regular ping of his phone. "Haven't heard from him in a while. Think he's busy at work."

Bigsy grunted and picked up his bass guitar, happy now he knew the source of Finn's sulking wasn't anything sinister. "Won't know unless you ask. Get him over to watch the footie on Saturday. Gonna be a good one."

"You think?"

"Why not? Trust me, mate. Don't rely on fate to sort your shit out, 'cause all that happens is bloody nothing."

"Are we talking about something else now?" Bigsy was a man with a lot on his plate: wife, kids, and, since the death of his mother, parental responsibility for a wild-child younger sister. "How's Gemma? Hasn't been nicked again, has she?"

"Hmm? Oh, not for a while. She was talking about college the other day, if you can believe it."

"That's good." Bigsy's sister was the bane of his life. Last Finn had heard, he'd had to change the locks on his house to stop her sneaking in and cleaning him out. "Is she clean?"

Bigsy grunted. "Doubt it. Reckon she's got a long way left to fall before that happens."

Finn let it go. Bigsy had a heart of gold, but he was a private kind of bloke, and talking about his family, fractured so often by death and heartache, didn't come easy to him. "All right, mate. Let's take it again from the bridge."

LATER THAT night, Finn went home to an empty house, and as had become his habit in recent days, ate some dinner, showered, then took to his bed to stare at his phone. Bigsy had been right. Danny hadn't sent more than a cursory text in days, but there was nothing stopping Finn from ringing him up, right?

Yeah. Right. Nothing except his loudest demons telling him Danny's silence was a subliminal message.

Fuck that.

Finn clicked on Danny's number before he could second-guess himself. The call connected on the third ring. He heard a muffled curse before Danny came on the line, gruff and irritated.

"Yeah?"

Finn sat up in bed, paradoxically caught off guard. "You really do sound miles away this time."

"Finn?"

"Yep." Finn hugged his knees to his chest. "I was worried I'd made you up, so I figured I'd give you a call."

A beat of silence, then a gentle huff of air. "Shit. Sorry I haven't called. It's been a heavy week. I haven't been home since Wednesday."

"You sound knackered."

"I am…." Danny broke off and yawned. "But enough about me. How are you? I'm sorry I ran out on your gig. It was ace, by the way. Can't remember if I got round to telling you."

Finn smiled and relaxed a little. Something about his feelings for Danny made his stomach churn in a way that wasn't entirely pleasant, but this… lying in bed with Danny's voice in his ear… yeah, he could do this all night. "I can't remember either. Seems so long ago, I can't believe it's only been a week."

"A lot can happen in a week, I s'pose. What are you up to now? Anything fun?"

Finn snorted. "Not really. I'm in bed by myself. That's never fun."

"Bed sounds good, though."

"When do you get to go home?"

"In the morning." Danny yawned again. He really did sound exhausted, and Finn felt bad for doubting him. "I'm in the car right now. Good job you called, actually. I was dozing off."

"Are you driving?"

"Nah, just waiting."

"Like a stakeout?"

Danny laughed. "Something like that, only far less exciting."

Curiosity burned a hole in Finn's shambolic brain, but Danny's vague answer told him further questioning would get him nowhere. "So… it's the Liverpool derby on Saturday.

Most of the band are watching it here. Come over if you want."

Silence, one of those awkward, stretched-out beats that amplified the noise in Finn's subconscious until he was sure he'd made a total twat of himself. Then a car door slammed on the street outside the house, and he realized he'd zoned out and missed Danny's answer. "Huh?"

Danny chuckled. "I said I'll come over if I get off work in time."

There wasn't much else to say. Finn said good-bye and hung up, then lay back on his bed and stared at the ceiling. He'd felt adrift all week, but Danny's gently dry humor had evened him out.

The front door banged. Jack was home, and he wasn't alone. Finn listened to him and Will crash around, pretended to be asleep when Jack checked on him, then later, heard them slip into bed and fuck. Hearing them love each other like that often pissed Finn off as much as he felt happy for them, but tonight, with Danny's warm laugh echoing in his head, he found comfort in their affection and fell asleep.

JACK FLICKED a balled-up crisp packet at Finn's head. "Piss off with the Morcheeba, will you?"

"Fuck off." Finn threw a glare in Jack's general direction, knowing it would only encourage Jack to wind him up more.

"Seriously, mate. You only play that stoner shite when you're nervous. Why are you so agitated about this bloke coming over? Thought you'd shagged him already."

"Fuck *off*." Finn looked around for something else to throw.

Will intervened. "Jack, leave him alone. Just 'cause you don't give a shit what I think of you, doesn't mean everyone else is the same."

"Bollocks. That's not true." Jack looked affronted, but Will had him there. The two of them had been friends their whole lives. They knew each other inside out, loved each other flaws and all, even if they weren't always sure what to do with it.

Finn gave Jack the finger and went back to his Gibson. The match had started half an hour ago, and Finn's house was full of the friends who made his life bearable—made his life *happy* —but with Danny due anytime, his nerves had got the better of him and he'd retreated to the dining room. Jack had come after him, and naturally Will had followed, so Finn's sanctuary had turned into Jack heckling him and Will doing his best to keep the peace.

Jack stomped off to find more crisps. Will took his place, perched on the battered dining table that held Jack's drum kit more often than it did plates of food.

"Play 'Big Calm' again. I like that one. Reminds me of Newquay Festival last year."

Finn strummed the warm chord pattern and smiled. Jack had taken Will all over the world with his DJ work, but the glitz and glamor was lost on Will. Finn too, for that matter, and for a while he let the grungy, mellow tune work its magic and calm the devil inside him.

Then he sensed a new presence and his world narrowed to the inky-haired man in the doorway. *He came.* Finn dropped his guitar pick. Danny came forward and retrieved it. He held it out with a tired smile.

"Don't stop. I like that one."

"Yeah?" Finn picked out the tune again. "Didn't have you pegged as a nineties trip-hop folk fan."

"A what?"

"Never mind."

Finn set his guitar aside. He felt vulnerable without its comforting weight in his hands, but the feeling faded as he and Danny stared at each other. True to his word, Danny looked like he hadn't slept in days, but Finn reckoned he'd never looked better.

"Er, on that note…." Will slid off the table and ducked around Danny. "I'm gonna find Jack."

Will disappeared. Danny shut the door behind him. "You look surprised. Forget you invited me over?"

"No, just wasn't sure you'd come."

"You keep saying that to me." Danny stepped closer and put his hands on Finn's shoulders. "Don't know why, though. There's nowhere else I'd rather be right now."

Finn felt warm all over. "Not even asleep in your own bed?"

"Rather be in yours."

If Danny was trying to be seductive, he hid it well. The comment seemed heartfelt rather than dirty, and despite the buzz of attraction between them, Finn didn't mind. He slid his arms around Danny's waist and pulled him into a hug rather than the kiss he so desperately craved. "Later. The guys won't stick around after the game. Jack and Will are off to Paris, and the others have got wives to get home to."

"Sounds good." Danny held Finn tight for a long moment, and then he pulled away and tried to tame Finn's wayward hair. "Who's winning?"

"Hmm?"

"The match. My mate Kev's a Kopite. He'll do his nut if Everton wins."

Oh yeah. Football. Finn found his focus and gaffer taped it to the front of his brain. "One-nil Everton when I last looked. Want to go see?"

Danny shrugged. Finn took it as a yes and hopped down from the stolen bar stool he'd been sitting on. He started for the door, itching to grab Danny's hand. He settled for the ukulele.

The house Finn shared with Jack was big and old—four floors of bay windows, high ceilings, and drafty wooden floors. They'd never got round to fixing it up much, and instead kept warm by filling their home with friends and music. Finn stuck his head around the living room door to find every available sofa and floor space covered with a reclining man, beer in hand, gaze fixed on the flat-screen TV.

Finn kicked Bigsy's legs. "Shove up."

Bigsy made room for Danny on the couch and offered his hand. The rest of the band followed suit, then returned their attention to the match. Only Ben, the Lamps' part-time fiddle player, seemed to be occupied with something else.

Finn slouched on the arm of the sofa by Danny and peered over Ben's shoulder. "Why are you writing the bass line in a different key?"

"Shit. I'm not, am I?" Ben pulled his earbud out and stopped scribbling in the composition notebook that looked suspiciously like one of Finn's.

Finn took the notebook and flipped through the pages. "'Fraid so. A minor and D major. What the fuck are you trying to write?"

Ben grimaced. "The Christmas play for my sister's class. She got stuck with the nativity, and the only thing she could find at the school was a scratched backing CD and a bunch of untitled lyrics. I promised her I'd transpose it into something simple."

"On the piano?" Finn stuck Ben's earbud in his ear and listened. The plastic Muzak-style backing track set his teeth on edge. "When does she need it?"

"Next week. Thought I'd broken the back of it, but if I've written half of it in the wrong key, I'm fucked."

"Then you should've asked Finn in the first place," Jack said without tearing his gaze from the football match. "He wrote the nativity for the New London Children's Choir a few years back."

"You did?" Ben looked surprised, and Finn could hardly blame him. It wasn't exactly rock-star stuff.

Finn shrugged and began rewriting the mess Ben had made of his bass clef key. "I didn't write the play—just the music. I was in the Priory, and they wouldn't let me have my

69

guitar. My mum convinced them kids' music was good for me."

That shut Ben up. Finn's illness was no secret, but it didn't come up in conversation much. Only Jack—and lately Will—could talk about it without averting his gaze.

Finn sensed Danny looking at him. He held up the music pad so Danny could see it. "You used to play, didn't you? Reckon you could bodge that?"

Danny snorted. "No chance."

"Come on," Finn needled. "You didn't even look."

Danny rolled his eyes but looked closer at the page of pencil-scratched notes. "Maybe the first few bars. You'd lose me here, though."

He pointed at the middle section. Finn frowned and studied the sequence of notes. He made some adjustments and held the pad up again, but Danny's attention had been diverted by Bigsy.

"Where are you from, mate? Are you Japanese or something?"

"Cardiff," Danny said. "My mum's Chinese, though. She came over from Beijing with my nan in the seventies."

Bigsy grunted, filed the information away, and went back to the football, but his curiosity had reminded the others there was a stranger in their midst.

Fred, the occasional rhythm guitarist, looked Danny over. "You've got proper straight hair, mate. Finn, who was that bloke used to play accordion for you, with the portable straighteners in his pocket? He'd fucking kill for hair like that."

"Cory." Finn scribbled a few notes. "He was with that girl who worked in Asda, but I swear he was gayer than me."

Fred sniggered and the moment passed. Finn finished the page of composition. He was about to flip to the next when he felt Danny shift and realized Danny was in a world of his own.

Finn nudged him. "All right?"

The words were mouthed and silent, but Danny looked startled all the same. Finn took pity on him. Danny didn't seem to have much more interest in football than Finn. "Come downstairs. I want to show you something."

They slipped away from the living room with little commotion. Only Jack seemed to notice them leaving. Finn led Danny down the cellar stairs and opened the door to the only place in the house—sometimes the only place at all—he could truly call his own. Unless he was fritzing out and needed help, no one else ever ventured down there.

Danny took in the racks and racks of instruments and musical paraphernalia, and the bright, colorful walls. "It's like Aladdin's cave down here."

Finn grinned. "That's the idea. I got it soundproofed when I bought the house. I just need a fridge and a bog and I'd never come out."

Danny caught the hidden reference. "This is your safe place."

It wasn't a question, and Danny didn't seem to expect an answer. He drifted to the back wall and squinted at the only platinum disc Finn had ever put up. "Bloody hell. You wrote the soundtrack to *Dead Beat Soul*?"

"Yep." Finn felt a faint warmth flush his cheeks. *Dead Beat Soul* was an indie cult film that had hit the big time, and perhaps the work he was most proud of.

"Fucking hell." Danny shook his head. "More to you than meets the eye, eh?"

"If you say so." Finn reckoned it was probably the other way around. Danny had an honest smile, but Finn still felt like he knew nothing about him.

"Are you going to help Ben with the rest of that nativity?"

"Help? Nah, I'll probably just end up writing it for him." Finn gave in to temptation and wound his arms around Danny from behind. "You could be my test case. See if you can play my pieces."

"That would be a pretty short experiment."

71

"That's what Will said when I started teaching him, but he played keyboards at every festival we played last summer."

"Festivals?" Danny leaned into Finn and closed his eyes. "I used to like festivals. Haven't been to one in years, though."

"Easily fixed."

Finn left it at that. Danny seemed to be pondering something, and Finn was content to make himself at home in the crook of Danny's neck until he'd figured it out.

LATER THAT afternoon, Finn finally forced himself to stop molesting Danny. "I'm hungry."

Danny laughed. "You just ate a jumbo sausage roll."

"That was ages ago." On cue Finn's stomach rumbled, a forlorn and empty sound, like it knew his fridge contained nothing but raw chicken, beer, and a jar of pickled onions. "Maybe we should go out."

Danny raised his head from Finn's chest. "Out?"

"Yeah. My fridge is bare and there are no decent takeaways around here."

Danny sat up. "How bare is your fridge? Bet it's not as hopeless as you think."

Finn took the challenge and let Danny haul him off the couch, where they'd been messing around since the rest of the guys had left.

They shuffled into the kitchen, Danny attached to Finn from behind, arms around him, lips in that devilish hollow behind Finn's ear. Danny pointed at a photo of Finn and Jack on the fridge door. "When was that taken?"

Finn looked closer at the image of him jumping on Jack's back while Will looked on, bemused. "Glasto '05, so six years ago. We'd only just met that day."

"You look so young."

"I was young. I was twenty-one."

Danny pondered that a moment, perhaps counting back the years to work out if Finn had been diagnosed by that point. Finn wondered if he'd have the same reaction most others did when they figured out Finn had been living with schizophrenia for two years by the time that photo was taken.

But you look so happy. Finn stifled a long repressed growl of frustration. *I am happy, goddammit.*

Danny opened the fridge. "You've got chicken."

Finn rolled his eyes. "There's fuck all else."

"Liar." Danny rummaged around the neglected vegetable drawer. "You've got garlic and ginger. Is there any rice?"

"Dunno. Have a look."

Danny let go of Finn and opened a few cupboards. "You've got loads of food. Look, you've got three types of rice."

That was news to Finn. His kitchen was big on fry-ups, toast, and bizarre gadgets no one ever used. He watched Danny retrieve a few other things and a pan and set it all out on the side. "Those stock cubes aren't mine. You bought them when you made that roast dinner."

Danny grinned. "I remember, and I also remember how pants your cooking skills were. Come here. Maybe *I* can teach *you* something."

Turned out he could. Chicken, rice, ginger, and soy sauce became Nana Wu's magic one-pot dish, and just about the best thing Finn had ever eaten.

After, Finn washed up and wandered into the living room to find Danny asleep on the couch. Finn crouched by his side and considered pulling a blanket over him and leaving him to it, but the house got cold at night, and the lure of coaxing Danny into his bed was too strong to ignore.

He tapped Danny's cheek until his eyes fluttered open. "Wanna go to bed?"

"Hmm?" Danny blinked sleepily. "Shit, did I conk out on you?"

"Little bit."

Danny sat up. "I should go."

"Working tomorrow?"

"Hope not—"

Finn cut Danny off with a kiss that felt lazy and rousing, all mixed together in a crazy pot of something he'd never felt before. "Then stay."

Danny didn't take much persuading. Finn guided him upstairs, pushed him down on the bed, and straddled him, clothes long forgotten, littering the stairs.

They kissed, biting and bruising. Finn felt Danny hard beneath him, pressing… wanting, and, fuck, Finn wanted him too. They grappled and rolled a few times. Finn found himself close to the bedside table and grabbed what they needed.

Danny lay on his back, hands behind his head, legs parted, watching as Finn squeezed lube on his fingers. He looked so relaxed Finn wondered what would happen if he eased his fingers into Danny instead of himself. If he rolled the condom on his own cock and drove inside Danny….

Wow. It was a thought Finn couldn't finish, and one, perhaps, for another day. He climbed over Danny and kissed him, absorbing his gasp as he slid down, slow and sure, inch by inch, until there was nothing between them but heaving chests and stuttered gasps.

Finn waited for his body to accept the burning intrusion. He hid his face in Danny's neck and counted his breaths.

Danny rubbed his back. "Okay?"

Finn rocked his hips in answer, and the pain dulled to an amber warmth that wrapped around his spine and spread like creeping wildfire.

Danny sucked in a harsh breath and gripped Finn's hips. Finn bit his lip. He'd learned Danny was a quiet lover… but lethal, and it wasn't long before Finn's dominance faded and Danny had him undone.

Finn held the headboard as Danny thrust up into him. Bottoming always turned him inside out, but Danny was something else, the way he dug his fingers into Finn's back, pulled him down, and held him in an embrace so tight Finn could hardly breathe. Finn couldn't count his sexual partners, never tried, but he'd never been with anyone who'd held him as close as Danny. Never felt so wanted, even just for a moment.

He'd never come so quick either, or so hard and out of the blue. A brush of Danny's hand was all it took, and Finn was done. White spots danced in his eyes and he cried out into the crook of Danny's neck.

Danny picked up the pace. He slammed into Finn over and over, forcing every pulse and tremor from him before he stilled and Finn felt a rush of heat where they were joined.

"*Fuck.*" Danny's exclamation was growly and low, but the flush on his chest gave him away.

Finn shivered, though not from cold. How could he be cold with Danny's arms around him? "That was epic."

Danny hummed. Finn climbed off him and made a quick, halfhearted effort to clean up. But not quick enough. Danny was fast asleep by the time he came back to bed. Finn drew the duvet up the bed and burrowed as close to Danny as he dared without waking him up. Danny looked different when he slept—younger… freer. Finn traced his high cheekbones and perfect skin, kissed his ink-black hair, and fell asleep dreaming of what life would be like if he had Danny in his bed forever.

CHAPTER EIGHT

DANNY STOOPED and scrutinized the dead girl on the autopsy table, equal parts apathetic, sickened, and oddly fascinated. It had always struck him strange how the skin of a human cadaver became almost translucent. He'd never seen anything else like it. The blue-gray color was a shade unique to the dead, and it had haunted his dreams for weeks after he'd seen his first corpse.

He straightened up. The dead girl looked familiar, but her faded characteristics didn't match up with any of the toms in his notes. "Can you tell if she'd had intercourse before she died?"

"There were no traces of semen, but she has scars and abrasions that suggest she had frequent, multiple partners."

The pathologist remained impassive, like he'd seen it all before. Perhaps he had. And Danny was beginning to feel the same. The young redhead was the second dead prostitute in as many weeks, and though the women had been found two miles apart and there was still no evidence to suggest foul play, there *were* some similarities—age, build, the place they'd been found. Coincidence, perhaps, but Danny's gut whispered not. What were the chances of two toms lying down in a ditch and dying of natural causes?

"You're sure she didn't OD?" Danny asked.

"Sure as I can be. She had high levels of heroin and barbiturates in her system, but not enough to kill a hardened addict."

That was good enough for Danny until he heard otherwise. The pathologist was approaching retirement and one of the best in the business. There wasn't much he hadn't seen.

Danny bade him good-bye and left the morgue, a depressing place at the best of times, let alone before breakfast on a Monday morning. And even now he'd seen the body, he didn't have much to go on. It had hardly been worth the predawn freak show, and it definitely hadn't been worth leaving Finn in bed.

Danny walked back to his car, half his mind still on the dead girl and the other in that cozy place he reserved for Finn. That place where it was all too easy to forget the outside world existed, at least until the phone had rung at 5:00 a.m., summoning him to the mortuary. Waking Finn so early had proved no easy feat, and Danny still wasn't convinced he'd understood why Danny had left him in bed.

Left him *naked* in bed….

Danny suppressed a shiver that had nothing to do with the frosty morning air, fished his phone from his pocket, and tapped out a message: *Sorry I snuck out on u. Work. Ring u latr*

He didn't expect a response anytime soon. It was still only just past seven, and Finn had been out of it when Danny had left him. He was a little startled when his phone flashed before he could drop it back in his pocket.

Thought I'd dreamt you.

Danny frowned. The comment would be benign from anyone else, but from Finn….

His phone buzzed again before the thought got away from him.

In the studio till late. Mite not hear phone. Ring u when I'm done.

Danny's heart gave a little flutter. Somehow Finn always made a simple phone call something to look forward to.

He pocketed the phone and wove his way through the early morning traffic. He reached his desk at 8:00 a.m. and hardly had time for a cuppa before the DCI came looking for him.

"My office, Danny."

Good morning to you too. Danny abandoned his tea, followed the DCI into his office, and shut the door. Most of CID would know about the latest dead girl by now, but he doubted anyone had seen the memo from Manchester, and he wanted to keep it that way until he'd established a cause of death for both women.

The DCI poured himself a coffee from the well-stocked machine in the corner. He offered Danny a mug as an afterthought.

Danny waved it away. Coffee made him jumpy. "I've brought the pathologist's preliminary notes back with me. Not much to go on. They put a rush on the toxicology tests, but the level of junk in her is consistent with a long-term addict."

"COD? Rape? Defense wounds?"

"Cause of death is inconclusive," Danny said, and then he repeated the briefing he'd received from the pathologist.

The DCI said nothing for a moment, and then he sighed. "And no ID either. What happens to these people that they can just disappear and no one notices?"

Danny didn't answer. It felt a little late for the DCI to begin empathizing with the toms on his patch. "I'm going to canvas some squats today. See if anyone's missing a mate. I'll head out tonight too."

"Good idea. Take Lanes. If this turns into something, you'll need someone decent with you."

Danny nodded. Jen Lanes was a good detective, and he'd worked with her before. "Was there anything else?"

"Actually, yes." The DCI opened a drawer and retrieved

an issue of the *Manchester Evening News*. He tapped his finger on the main headline: "Street Girls Vanish." "The press knows something's up in Manchester. None of their missing persons have turned up dead yet, but if the media links them to ours, we're going to have a circus on our hands."

Danny agreed. He'd worked high-profile cases before—one of the cons of working Vice—and they were a nightmare. "One of ours could turn out to be theirs, though. We should touch base, at least."

"Okay. Do it. Samms is the bloke running their investigation. He's a bit of a bastard, but gets the job done. I'll forward you his contact details. In the meantime we need to hold a press conference here. Lay some foundations. You in?"

A press conference? Fuck that shit. "All due respect, guv, but I won't blend in out there if my face is all over the telly."

It was a genuine excuse Danny had used before, but the DCI wasn't fooled. "Bloody camera-shy youngsters. Think that lot don't get bored with my ugly mug all the time?"

Danny shrugged and escaped the office to round up Jen Lanes. It was going to be a long day, and the sooner they got started, the better.

DC JEN Lanes circled the small cordoned off area for a second time, then came to a stop by Danny and looked up the embankment. "No sign of a body being dragged."

Danny looked up from his position crouched on the ground, checking his notes against the forensic crew's assessment. "Yep. Looks like she died right here. Question is… how?"

"You think?" Lanes shot him a withering glare, and Danny answered with a wry grin. A crime scene was no place for glib jokes, but a little dark humor was always welcome in the middle of a long day. "How much did she weigh?"

"A little over eight stone."

Lanes whistled. "Not much, then. So she could've been carried here?"

"From the road?" Danny glanced over his shoulder at the busy dual carriageway. "Not without being seen, even at night. This is the main lorry route through Nottingham."

Lanes didn't look convinced, and that was what Danny liked about her. "A lorry could stop here for a few minutes and dump a body."

"Or there's a parking stop a mile north. She could've walked here…"

"…with whoever killed her," Lanes finished.

"We don't know anyone killed her yet," Danny said, but though the investigation hadn't produced any tangible evidence, instinct and plain old common sense told Danny there was no other reason for two vulnerable women to turn up dead in ditches, especially within a week of each other.

On cue his phone rang. The number for the pathologist's office flashed up on the screen. Danny beckoned Lanes closer while he listened to the updated report from the first body. When the pathologist was done, Danny thanked him and hung up. Then he clambered out of the ditch with Lanes hot on his heels and surveyed the busy road.

"Dead girl number one was asphyxiated. They're looking again at number two. Let's go back to your lorry-driver theory. If she was smothered too, we'll need all the hypotheses we can get."

LATER THAT night after a long day gathering route schedules from haulage firms and canvassing dirty squats, Danny left Lanes reviewing his carefully maintained notes on local toms and drove home via the red-light district. He cruised the streets for a while, calling over girls he recognized, checking in, testing the water. He was on his second pass of Lexi's stomping ground when a lone figure caught his attention, a tiny slip of a girl who looked like she had more business hanging around the local comprehensive than touting a street corner.

Danny checked for a pimp or a boyfriend lurking in the shadows, then pulled up and rolled his window down.

He beckoned the redhead over. She approached him with a nervous smirk that turned Danny's stomach.

"Looking for some company?"

"Nope." Danny flashed his warrant card. "DC Jones. Notts City CID. What are you doing out here?"

The girl scowled, adding weight to Danny's suspicion that she was underage. "Nothing. Just walking around. Not a pissing crime, is it?"

"Depends. How old are you?"

"Twenty-one."

"Pull the other one. Try again."

"Nineteen."

Danny wasn't convinced. "What's your name?"

"Jade."

Jade. Fuck's sake. How many toms called themselves that? "Got any ID, Jade?"

"Left it at home."

"Course you did. And where's home? You live around here?"

Jade shrugged and pointed vaguely behind her. "Up the road."

Danny considered his options—leaving her be, taking her home, busting her for soliciting—and none of them sat well. Taking her home was dubious. If she really did live in one of the dodgy bedsits up the road, rocking up with the old Bill could get her in trouble, and busting her was twattish and pretty much entrapment.

That left leaving her on the street to her fate.

Danny held out his contact card. "Go home. I'm working this beat tonight. If I see you again, I'll nick ya. Got it?"

"Yeah, yeah." Jade squinted at the card. "You don't look

like a Jones. You look like that bloke from the telly."

Danny put the car in gear. "If you're gonna tell me I look like Ken Hom, you can piss off. Go on, home with you. I don't want to see you again."

The girl tottered away in her plastic heels. Danny watched her in the rearview mirror until she disappeared into an alleyway, and then he pulled away from the curb and resumed his task of circling the red-light district.

It was just after midnight when a panda car pulled him over for curb crawling. "I've been out here for three hours," Danny said when he'd identified himself, "and you've only just noticed?"

"Piss off." The uniformed PC grinned. "Don't you think we've got better things to do than chase after johns all night?"

Danny rolled his eyes. DCI Brown's press conference had gone out that afternoon, but he hadn't identified the dead girls as prostitutes because they still didn't know they were. "McDonald's is that way. On a serious note, though, couldn't hurt to make the rounds a few times now you're here."

The beat coppers were agreeable enough, so Danny left them to it and drove home. He was halfway there when his phone rang.

Danny clicked the hands-free function without checking the caller ID, keeping his eyes on the road. "Yeah?"

There was no response—verbally, at least. Instead the sound of an acoustic guitar layered over a funky drum track filled the car. Danny smiled and let it seep into him. The gravelly tone of the vocals were very Finn, but the deep rhythm behind it sounded more like the chill-step stuff Danny had come to know as Jack's signature style, and the liquid beat combined with Finn's voice was just what he needed to hear.

The thought of Jack stopped him switching off completely, though, and as he navigated his way through the city, he recalled the dark words Jack had growled at him the day before when he'd answered Danny's knock on Finn's front door.

Finn's the nicest bloke in the world. Treat him right. You can't just say you're going to be there for him. You have to bloody do it.

Danny had stood his ground and stared Jack down. He'd seen too much shit to be intimidated by a belligerent kid, but he'd taken the warning to heart. Reconnecting with Finn had been awesome, but spending time with Finn's friends had brought home to Danny how restricted his own life was. Was it fair to bring Finn into that? Danny didn't think so. Crawling back in the closet had been a miserable experience he wouldn't wish on anyone, least of all a soul as bright as Finn.

A wave of hopelessness swept over Danny. Perhaps it was just fatigue, or the fact that he'd spent all day digging into the worst things human beings could do to each other and themselves, but driving through the night, surrounded by all that was Finn, Danny couldn't help pondering what the future held for them. Secrecy, late-night phone calls, and abandoned dates. Finn deserved better than that.

Didn't stop Danny enjoying the music, though, or quell the craving to see Finn play live again. Finn's music, in all its forms, held a certain kind of magic, and the mish-mash track kept Danny company all the way home until it cut out and the line went dead. The abrupt silence startled Danny enough to get out of his car and haul himself up the stairs of his building. He tapped out a message as he let himself into his flat: *Very Zero 7. U having a 90s throwback?*

Finn replied: *Maybe. Think Jack's been on the weed again, but I like it.*

I like it too.

U home?

Just got in.

Tired?

Fucked.

Get some kip. Call me 2morrow.

Danny smiled. *Try and stop me.*

CHAPTER NINE

FINN CROUCHED on the stage, jiggling the lead that connected the bass amp to the power supply. The rest of the band had long since lost patience and stomped back to the dressing room, leaving the broken amp to the road crew, but Finn persevered. The task gave him something to do and distracted him from preshow jitters he'd never quite learned to control, the nerves that made every show feel like the first.

The amp whistled, low at first, then loud enough to make Finn cringe, then it crackled and hissed and his persistence paid off. He picked up Bigsy's discarded bass guitar and ran through a few riffs, completing the sound check that had been interrupted by the amp's demise.

He got lost for a while. He hadn't played bass in ages, and Bigsy's guitar was awesome, especially when he was too grumpy to stick around and stop Finn playing it. The thicker strings were harder to manipulate, but Finn enjoyed the low, soulful rhythm until the doors to the venue opened and he made his escape backstage.

He found the band lounging around. None of them cared much for preshow rituals. Ben and Bigsy played cards in the corner, and Jack was on the couch, tapping a restless beat on his thigh, engrossed in something on his phone.

Finn stepped around him and retrieved his own phone from his coat pocket. He'd been checking it all day, hoping for a message from Danny, and this time he got lucky.

Play something for me….

Finn felt a pull in his chest. He hadn't seen Danny for more than a week, not since he'd woken alone with only a bed that smelled of Danny and sex to show Danny had ever been there at all. Danny had worked every day since, and by the time he'd had an evening free, Finn had been on his way to London for the Lamps' last run of gigs before they took a break over Christmas.

Finn shot a text back, wishing Danny was there to hear the song Finn had in mind for him. Danny was a reserved bloke, quiet… stoic, but there was no denying music got under his skin, and there was nothing Finn loved more than reeling Danny in… watching his eyes darken and his smile turn wistful. Sometimes Finn felt desperate to know what he was thinking, but others… nah. The smile was enough.

Half his mind back in bed with Danny, Finn glanced around the room again. The band was due on stage in fifteen minutes, but no one seemed to care. Instead the room had grown quiet and every man's gaze was trained on the TV, watching the nine o'clock news.

The news? Really? "What the fuck are you watching?"

No one answered. Finn looked to the screen to see what had captured his usually disinterested bandmates so entirely. An image of a local motorway bridge flashed up. A body of a young woman had been found beneath it. The cause of death was unknown, but by the massive police presence, Finn guessed she'd been murdered.

"It's the third one," Jack said to no one in particular. "They reckon it's a serial killer, like that bloke back in the eighties. What was his name?"

"Yorkshire Ripper," Ben said. "Or was it Jack the Ripper?"

"Same thing, innit?"

Finn rolled his eyes and kicked Bigsy's leg. "I don't give a fuck what he's called. Get your arses ready to go on stage."

"Don't kick me, you fucking twat. I'll knock your block off."

Finn bristled. Bigsy had been in a bad mood all day. "What's up with you?"

"Nothin'."

"Yeah? So why do you want to fight me?"

Bigsy's growly expression softened to reveal a weariness Finn hadn't noticed before. "Sorry, mate. Just got some family stuff pissing me off."

"Gemma giving you gip?"

"Wouldn't know. Haven't seen her in weeks."

Finn held out his hand and hauled Bigsy to his feet. "Anything I can do?"

"You're doing it, mate. Don't worry about me. I'll be okay once we get out there."

Two hours later Finn jumped off stage, sweaty, buzzed, ears ringing and his bones vibrating from the stamping feet of the ten-thousand-strong crowd. It had been their biggest gig of the year, selling out the Brixton venue, and it had been a banger. Finn had played an old Idlewild song for Danny alone on his acoustic guitar. One of the road crew had videoed it, a request the bloke had obviously thought odd since Finn usually avoided cameras like the plague.

Finn e-mailed the footage to Danny, then helped the roadies pack up the gear. Bigsy and the others were staying the night in London with their significant others, but Finn and Jack were driving home, both of them itching to get back to their men.

The band parted ways. The road crew took the sound equipment, leaving Finn with the instruments packed into the van. He looked around for Jack. It took him a while to find him puking his guts up in the backstage bathroom.

Finn's heart sank. Jack had suffered from crippling migraines for as long as Finn had known him. The affliction had briefly forced him out of the dance clubs and into the production studio, but he'd been on some nuclear medication for the past year or so, and the attacks had become so sporadic Finn had almost forgotten about them.

Almost.

Finn crouched and put his arm around Jack. He knew it was little comfort when Jack felt so rough, but there wasn't much else he could do. "Drugs will kick in soon, mate."

"Haven't got any. Ran out."

Jack pushed his forehead against his drawn-up knees. Finn rubbed the back of his neck, wishing he could do more.

"Have you got any at home?"

"No. The prescription's in my wallet. I forgot to get it filled."

Shit. Finn didn't know what to do. It was past midnight, too late for any pharmacies he knew of to be open. "Do you want to crash at the hotel across the road?"

It was the last thing on earth Finn wanted to do. He wanted to go home, send a dirty text to Danny, and sleep in his own bed. But he knew Jack: he needed a quiet, dark room, and the sooner, the better.

Thankfully Jack had other ideas. "Nah. Fuck that. Let's go home. I can get the prescription at that all-night Tesco in Arnold."

Or not. Jack was in no state to endure the all-night supermarket in one of the roughest parts of Nottingham, with its bright lights and hordes of late-night shoppers and junkies. Finn would have to do it for him, and despite the challenges he set himself daily, he hadn't been in a big supermarket in years.

Finn helped Jack up and walked him to the van, keeping an eye out for lurking photographers. Jack was the most well-known of them all, and getting caught staggering out of a venue, no matter the reason, was a hassle he didn't need.

Finn navigated the north circular while Jack got his head down beside him, then they hit the M1…. No music, no conversation, just a silence that got under Finn's skin and latched on to his unsettled nerves.

It took all his concentration to stay on the road… to ignore the whispering voice in his head, the one that popped up from time to time like it had never gone away, like it had always been there. The one that told him he was about to lose it and drive him and Jack off the road, killing them both. Or worse—killing Jack and living with Will's grief.

Get a grip. Finn clenched the steering wheel. Years of living with schizophrenia had taught him that often his most frightening thoughts were nothing more than anxiety, but the times when they hadn't been… the times when they'd become his worst nightmares, when he'd been trapped in his own head, too fucked up to reason his way out…. Fuck, those times haunted him. Haunted him enough to make his heart beat faster and his palms sweat. Enough for his breath to get stuck in his throat, and his teeth to bite down on his lip so hard he tasted blood.

He zoned out so much he almost missed the junction for Nottingham. The sudden swerve into the exit lane roused Jack.

"Where are we?"

"Junction 26." Finn pulled up at a light-controlled roundabout. "Are you going to be sick again?"

Jack grunted and sat up, his hand hovering over his mouth. "I'm all right."

He didn't look all right, and when Finn parked up outside the all-night Tesco, he felt like he might throw up himself. "Where's your prescription slip?"

Jack fumbled in his pocket and retrieved a crumpled sheet of paper from his wallet. "You don't have to come in with me."

Finn steeled himself and plucked the prescription from Jack's unsteady hands. "Just stay here, yeah? And don't puke in the van."

He got out before Jack could protest and took an uncertain step toward the huge automatic doors. The nasty voice in his head struck up a tune, a dark, ominous melody that told him he wouldn't take another step, and for a moment, Finn gave in. Jack could sleep this off, right? He had before, and the morning wasn't so far away.

Or Will could go…. *Or you could just stand here all fucking night while Jack suffers alone….*

Finn took a shuddery breath and reached for a song to beat back the voice. He found the last song he'd played that night, and Danny's face flashed into his mind, steady and calm. Finn felt Danny's dark gaze on him. Felt him watch Finn's fingers dance over the guitar, absorbing every note like Finn had played it just for him. Of course, that night Finn had. The song he'd sung for Danny was old and rough, and the lyrics didn't quite fit, but the tone had suited his mood and matched the nagging worry that, despite Danny's growing presence in Finn's life, something unseen stood between them. Danny was distracted, and not knowing why bugged Finn more than he cared to admit.

Didn't stop him using Danny's smile to force himself forward, though. One step, two steps, three. Then he was inside and the lights and noise hit him like walking out on stage, only without the shield of his guitar and the heady rush of music to protect him.

Finn looked up at the signs hanging from the ceiling. The pharmacy was at the back of the store. To get there, he needed to push his way through the aisles, half blocked by huge cages of goods being stacked on the shelves.

Great. If this was what these places were like at midnight, Finn shuddered to think what they were like in daylight. Actually he just shuddered, one of those invisible convulsions that felt like his brain had been zapped with electrodes.

He made it to the pharmacy. The woman behind the counter gave him a pen and then waited, staring, while he signed his name as Jack's representative.

Finn tried to ignore the creeping sensation her attention gave him. Paranoia. He'd learned to live with it, but it didn't get any easier. People often stared at him like they couldn't quite place him. Some days he thought life would be easier if he'd let himself become a clichéd rock-star wanker. At least then he'd *know* why people were looking at him.

A few minutes later, he fled the counter, paper bag in hand. A stop at the cigarette counter for a bottle of water about finished him off, and he drifted back to the car on shaky legs.

Jack stared at him with hazy eyes. "You're a real mate, you know that?"

Finn said nothing. It hurt to know Jack knew exactly what going into that stupid bloody supermarket had done to him.

"Finn?"

"*What?*"

"Have you decided about the Big Chill next year?"

The random question caught Finn off guard, even though he knew Jack was making a valiant effort to distract him. "Why are you worried about that now?"

"I'm not worried. I just want to know."

Finn put the van in gear and reversed out of the parking space. The alternative dance festival was Jack's favorite event of the year. Finn had gone with him for as long as they'd been friends. Why would Jack think next year would be any different?

"You should bring Danny."

"Danny?"

Jack sat up a little, though Finn could see, even in his peripheral vision, how sick he still felt. "Yeah, Danny. He is your boyfriend, isn't he?"

Was he? The term didn't sit right in Finn's convoluted

mind right then. "I don't think Leftfield and poppers are his scene."

"Don't know till you ask, do you?"

But Finn did know. Danny was a copper. He wasn't going to sit around in a field smoking bloody weed. Not that Finn smoked weed… anymore.

"You're pretty cagey about him."

"That's bollocks." Finn kept his gaze on the road. It hadn't escaped his notice that Jack had been cool with Danny whenever they happened to cross paths, but that was standard practice for Jack and any man Finn brought home these days, not that there were many.

Jack said no more. Back at the house, he staggered straight upstairs and collapsed on his bed fully clothed. Finn stayed with him until the drugs knocked him out, then crept away to call Will—who, predictably, got straight in his car—then take a shower.

After, he found himself pacing the dark, silent house. Will was more than an hour away, and though Finn knew Jack was in no danger, he felt on edge. The usual postgig buzz had evaporated the moment he'd seen Jack's cloudy eyes and pale face, and in its place, Finn felt like the walls were closing in on him.

He opened the fridge, shut it again, then eyed the cellar door, wanting nothing more than to creep down to his sanctuary of music and color and hide from the black silence of the house, but he resisted. He had to wait until Will got there. He owed Jack far more than that.

Shit. Finn stopped in the middle of the kitchen and rubbed his face. It had been a long time since he had truly lost himself to the monster of schizophrenia, and even now he couldn't remember much of it, but he knew Jack had been there, that he'd *stayed* there until Finn hadn't needed him anymore.

Finn turned back to the fridge. In the darkness he could just about make out the photographs stuck to every available inch of brushed stainless steel. Finn's whole life was on that fridge: family, friends, the band. Good times. Happy days. Everything Finn needed to see when his grasp on reality failed. Only Danny was missing.

Danny, Danny, Danny. For the first time in hours, a thought felt good. Finn grabbed it, sank to the floor, back against the cupboards, and held on to it until a knock at the door startled the ever-loving shit out of him. The tapping was light, barely there if it was there at all, but Finn jumped a mile. Who the fuck was that? It was 2:00 a.m. and Will had a key.

Maybe he forgot it. Dickhead. Finn punctuated his internal growl by hauling himself from the kitchen floor and padding to the front door. A shape on the other side of the frosted glass moved, a shadow that looked nothing like Will's lanky frame.

Finn frowned and opened the door, half convinced he'd find nothing but empty milk bottles or the neighbor's cat. Instead he found Danny, or rather Danny's back as he walked away. "Danny?"

Finn's voice was hoarse from a gig that felt so long ago he'd almost forgotten about it, but Danny heard him. He turned with a slow smile… a smile that seeped into Finn's soul and warmed him from the inside out.

Finn closed the distance between them, ignoring the icy cold of the Victorian tiles beneath his feet. "What are you doing here?"

Danny didn't answer right away. He wrapped Finn in a tight hug and squeezed. Then he sighed and pulled back a little. "You shouldn't be out here. You've got wet hair."

Finn had forgotten about that too, and Danny's cool fingers grazing his scalp felt amazing. "What are you doing here?"

The repetition seemed to rouse Danny from his preoccupation with Finn's hair. "Long night. Found myself driving by. Did I wake you?"

"No. We haven't been home long."

"We?"

"Jack's upstairs. He's ill, though. Migraine. That's why all the lights are off."

"Ah. I thought you were asleep."

Finn shook his head. "Nah. Too wired."

"From the gig?"

"Something like that."

Danny sensed the heaviness Finn had unwittingly dropped on him. "What's up? You're shaking."

"Am I?" Was he? "You must have that effect on me."

Danny wasn't fooled. He pulled back a little and stared Finn down. "What's the matter?"

Finn didn't know how to answer that. He'd always tried to be open with his friends about the dark clouds that plagued him, but in his love life, honesty had often come back to bite him in the arse.

Danny touched his face. "Want to make me a brew?"

"Hmm?" Finn abruptly remembered they were standing on the porch, at the mercy of the icy wind. "Tea? Shit, yeah. Come in. We have to be quiet, though. Jack's ill."

"Migraine. Nasty. Come on, then. Let's go inside."

Danny guided Finn inside and shut the door behind them. The darkness enveloped them like a blanket, and this time, with Danny right there with him, Finn welcomed it, like it could cocoon them together.

He took a deep breath and centered himself. "Tea. Yeah. Come on."

Danny hovered close by while Finn made tea. He didn't say much, but that wasn't unusual, and Finn wasn't feeling up to banal small talk. With the tea brewed, Finn considered the kitchen table, then the couch in the next room, and dismissed them both.

"Drink this in bed?"

Danny grinned a little. "There goes my flying visit."

"Piss off. It's not like I'm gonna tie you to the bedposts. You can leave whenever you want."

Danny made a noise low in his throat—a grunt, a growl, Finn couldn't tell—and pointed at the stairs. "Up."

In Finn's room they left the door ajar to listen out for Jack and Will, then stripped down to T-shirts and boxers and huddled up in Finn's bed. Safe in Danny's arms, Finn felt his heartbeat slow and his mind quiet, and realized he'd been far more wound up than he'd thought. He took comfort in Danny's calm, quiet presence and his wickedly soothing touch, and it was a while before he raised his head from Danny's chest.

"Thanks. I needed that."

"S'all right. You looked a little rattled."

Rattled. *Rattler.* That was a good name for the imaginary blender in Finn's mind. "I hate it when Jack's ill. It changes him and it scares me."

"Why?"

Finn shifted. He was on his side, pressed against Danny, absorbing his warmth, their tea long forgotten. He searched for the words to explain himself, but none came.

"You can tell me, Finn. You don't have to hide it from me."

And so Finn did. He told Danny everything and found himself shaking again, firmly rooted in that horrible place between hot and cold, with Danny's touch the only thing that felt real.

Danny listened in silence until Finn got to the part about the supermarket, and then he took Finn's hand and squeezed it. "Did you manage to go in?"

"Yeah, near enough pissed myself, though. Then I came home and wound myself up so much I was about to climb in the fridge when you turned up."

Danny looked as though he wanted to smile. Instead he tucked Finn's hair behind his ears. He did that a lot. "I get it, I think."

Finn scowled. "I don't want you to get it. I don't want you to know how weird I am."

"Weird compared to what? Finn, you did everything you

needed to do. You drove Jack home, got his prescription, and put him to bed. What else did you expect from yourself? And it's not weird to hate crowded places, mate. Lots of people do. My mum only leaves the house to go to the Chinese center in town. My dad does everything else for her."

"You never talk about your family."

"There isn't much to say."

Finn didn't believe that. "Do you ever see your sister?"

"Not as much as I should."

Danny wasn't much of a talker unless they were talking about music or food… or Finn, and Finn didn't have enough coherent thought to press him now.

Finn slid his hand under Danny's T-shirt. Danny's chest was smooth and strong, his heartbeat steady. "I think about you all the time."

It wasn't quite what he'd intended to say, but fuck, he meant it. He hadn't known Danny long… a month or so, but Finn couldn't imagine life without him now. When had that happened?

You pissing idiot. Half a dozen bunk-ups and you're mated for life? Daft fucking tw—

Danny's mouth came down on Finn's. It was a gentle kiss, but firm and demanding. Silencing. It took Finn's breath away and purged his mind of all else. Danny's lips. Danny's tongue. Danny putting his hands on Finn's shoulders, breaking the kiss and turning him so his back pressed against Danny's chest.

Finn arched into Danny's touch, felt Danny hard, pressing against his spine, and God, it felt good. "But Will's… not here… *fuck*!"

Danny tugged Finn's hair and nipped his neck. "We'll hear him… if you're quiet."

Quiet? Nope. Finn was a noisy lover and proud of it, but with Jack in the next room and the doors open, bearing Danny's teasing touch in silence became his only option.

Danny massaged Finn's clenched muscles until he quivered for all the right reasons, and then he pushed Finn forward and slid his lips and tongue down his spine, kissing, nipping, easing the tension out of Finn with every touch.

He stopped when he came to Finn's waistband. "How quiet do you think you can be?"

The gravelly whisper made Finn squirm and press his face into his pillow. He raised his hips and let Danny strip him of his remaining clothes. Then he lay there, facedown and prone, at Danny's mercy.

Danny gripped Finn's hips and parted his legs. He blew warm air over Finn, and Finn shuddered. He could imagine Danny's intentions well enough, but waiting for it was fucking torture. Until it happened, and then torture took on a whole new meaning. It had been ages since he'd last been rimmed. For Finn, there was nothing more intimate, and the sweep of Danny's tongue was so light and gentle he wanted to cry. Maybe he *did* cry a little. Danny had done strange things to Finn's heart since the moment they'd met.

Finn buried his face in the pillow, bit down, and clenched his fists. The pleasure was intense, not enough to make him come, but enough to make him scream, silent and unheard, except in his own head.

Danny kissed his way up Finn's spine and wound his arms around Finn's waist, naked… his skin a furnace against Finn's. When had that happened? Finn hadn't noticed Danny taking his clothes off.

Finn turned his head and found Danny's lips. The kiss was rough and dirty, belying the featherlight dance of Danny's fingertips on Finn's chest. Finn gasped, breathless and desperate, though for what, he didn't quite know. He just wanted… needed Danny, and he needed him now.

Danny let go and fumbled in Finn's bedside table. Cool air hit Finn's bare skin. Finn shivered. His body burned, but without Danny's attention, his mind started to wander. He heard a sound downstairs, a creaking pipe, perhaps. Or maybe Will's foot on the stairs. Finn hadn't heard the front door, but Danny's touch was like that... distracting, consuming.

Like he'd heard Finn's errant thoughts, Danny coaxed Finn onto his side so Finn could see the door. "I'll hear him."

It didn't escape Finn's notice that Danny had said "I," not "we," like he knew Finn was beyond such things, but Finn couldn't bring himself to care. Danny slipped into place behind him and brushed Finn's sweat-dampened hair back from his face.

"Okay?" Finn nodded, but Danny gripped his chin and forced him to meet his gaze. "Sure?"

"I'm sure." So fucking sure. Sex was no cure for schizophrenia, but as Finn yielded to Danny and let the burning sting of Danny's cock seep through him, he felt the demons fade and slip away into their locked box, like Danny had passed him the key.

Danny fucked Finn slowly, his arms tight around Finn, his lips at his neck. The encounter felt sweeter than any they'd shared before, and Finn felt liquid and boneless, even as he spilled over Danny's fist, his cry muffled by Danny's other hand, pressed gently over his mouth.

It took Finn a while to regain his faculties. Behind him, he was dimly aware of Danny moving around, clearing up, reclaiming the duvet that had somehow found its way to the floor, and draping it over Finn.

Danny slid back into bed. "Jesus. You're *still* shaking."

"Mmm. Feels good." Danny didn't answer. Finn opened a heavy eye to find Danny staring at him in the darkness, leaning over his shoulder, like Finn was an unexploded bomb. "What's wrong?"

"Nothing, mate. We're all right."

Finn frowned. *We're all right.* What the hell did that mean? He started to ask, but Danny shook his head.

"Shh. Go to sleep. I'll listen out for Jack until Will gets here."

CHAPTER TEN

DANNY WOKE to Finn's elbow in his face, and then the awkwardness of Finn trying to peel their sweat-sex-stuck bodies apart and sit up.

Finn mumbled something. Dazed, Danny rolled back and gave him some room.

"It's buzzing," Finn said.

"What is?"

"The bass amp."

Danny frowned and squinted in the darkness. They hadn't been asleep long, an hour or so, and his brain took a moment to compute. "Is it plugged in?"

"I need to jiggle the wire."

"Okay." Danny looked around for the errant amp. "Where is it?"

Finn didn't answer. He swung his legs out of bed, then stopped, like he couldn't remember what he was doing. "Why didn't you tune it when we got here?"

"What?"

"Shit breaks. If you'd tuned your bass, we'd have known the amp was broken hours ago."

Danny felt suddenly cold. He sat up and laid a cautious hand on Finn's arm. "Finn?"

Finn turned his head in the wrong direction and got up. He drifted to the window and fiddled with the catch. "I'll get them, Jack. Just stay here, yeah? I'll get them."

Fuck. Danny sprang out of bed and caught Finn's hands in his. "Finn? What are you doing, mate?"

Danny's voice seemed to throw Finn. He frowned, and close up, Danny saw his gaze was all wrong. *Is he even awake?* Danny had no idea. Sleepwalking seemed bad enough, but the alternative… shit. A ripple of fear lanced Danny's heart. Finn had never got round to telling him what to do if he was unwell.

"Come on." Danny tugged on Finn's arm. "Jack's asleep in bed. Will too. I heard him come home. Come back to bed."

It felt like leading a child away from a sweet shop at first. Finn planted his feet stubbornly on the floorboards, and it was all Danny could do to coax him away from the window, but then, halfway across the room, Finn's resistance evaporated. He dropped his arms, bypassed Danny, and slid back into bed like he'd always been there.

Danny stood alone in the dark for a long moment, staring. A sliver of moonlight filtered through the half-open curtains and caught Finn's skin so perfectly it didn't seem real. Nothing seemed real. Did that really just happen? Or had Danny's hellish week finally caught up with him?

No answer was forthcoming, from Finn, the moon, or Danny's subconscious, and eventually it got too cold to stand naked in the middle of Finn's drafty bedroom. Danny retrieved his boxers from the floor and tiptoed to the bathroom. On the way he shot a surreptitious glance through Jack's open door. He'd been telling the truth when he told Finn he heard Will let himself in and creep upstairs, and he looked at them now, curled up on Jack's bed, Will holding Jack's head on his chest, hands tangled his hair, and Danny felt a sudden deep-rooted need to take the quickest piss known to man and get back to Finn.

Finn hadn't moved when Danny got back. Danny crawled

in beside him and persuaded him to roll over. Finn let out a soft sigh and lolled his head on Danny's shoulder. It wasn't quite the tight embrace going on next door, but it was enough for Danny.

He held Finn for a long time and stared hard at him, like he could see through his skull and decipher the chaos in his brain. When that failed and sleep evaded him, he let his mind wander. Seeing Finn sleepwalk had scared the shit out of him and brought him back to reality with an unwelcome jolt. Finn had been rattled—trembling, muttering, distracted—when Danny arrived the night before, but it had faded as he'd lain in Danny's arms, and Danny put it down to his impromptu supermarket trip. He'd never understand how something he perceived as mundane could frighten Finn so much, but frighten Finn it did, and now, even with Finn sleeping so peacefully beside him, Danny couldn't help the nagging fear that he might have missed an ominous sign of something far, far worse.

Danny sighed. He needed to talk to Jack, but in the oppressive darkness, he could well imagine how that conversation would go.

Nice one, mate. Sex as therapy? What the fuck were you thinking?

Danny didn't have an answer to that, and the hopeless sensation took him back to the hellish shift that had brought him to Finn's doorstep in the first place. Body number three had brought Danny an eighteen-hour day and the near certainty he was dealing with multiple murders. Pathology results on two of the women were still inconclusive, but Danny *knew*… like every copper did: they were hunting a monster. The investigation was now the biggest he'd ever worked on, and the pressure on the whole team to produce a quick result was huge. But for Danny it felt like more than that. He'd watched over the toms since he'd joined the squad, and the responsibility to protect them now consumed him.

Only Finn held his heart more.

Danny closed his eyes and sighed. Finn needed him, he knew that, but girls were dying on his patch, and even though the DCI had ordered him to take twenty-four hours off, Danny couldn't find rest.

Eventually he gave up. He left Finn sleeping and crept downstairs and out to his car. He retrieved his laptop from the boot and brought it inside. In the quiet darkness of the house, he considered setting up shop at the kitchen table, but the pull to Finn was too strong. Instead he slipped back into bed, rearranged Finn, and opened his computer on his lap. He logged into his e-mail and pulled up the notes he'd saved on unsolved murders in the north of England, particularly those involving prostitutes. Most of the missing girls in Manchester had turned up one way or another, but two girls remained missing, and body number one had been confirmed as a Manchester-based tom.

A few details caught his attention. He highlighted them and then came back to one that had stuck out. A Derbyshire schoolgirl in the nineties… sixteen years old, raped and murdered on her way home from a friend's party. Her body had been found in a layby on Boxing Day, 1996, and her killer was never caught. Danny pulled up a map and traced the route between Nottingham and Derbyshire, a short buzz on the M1. The unsolved murder was fifteen years old, but something about it screamed at Danny. Was it the hair? The murdered schoolgirl had a distinctive copper bob cut. Danny pulled up the macabre images of the three more recent victims. To say they were all redheads was a stretch, but still… there was *something* about them all Danny couldn't put his finger on.

With a bad taste in his mouth, Danny went through his mental list of local toms and began the harrowing task of highlighting those he thought most at risk. At the top of his list were Lexi and the new girl on the block, Jade. He hadn't seen Lexi in a week or so, which wasn't unusual, but Jade was another story. After the first time, Danny had spotted her every time he'd driven the red-light district, but he hadn't seen her for the past few days, and though Lexi had been out of sight for longer, the absence of the young, willowy teenager bothered Danny more.

"What are you doing?"

"Hmm?" Danny glanced at Finn, surprised to find him wide-awake at 7:00 a.m., and closed his laptop, hoping Finn hadn't seen anything that would give him nightmares. "Nothing that can't wait. You all right?"

Finn put his chin on Danny's chest. "Think so. Sorry for fritzing out on you last night."

"S'okay. Do you feel better?"

"Yeah." Finn didn't say any more. He rolled out of bed, threw some clothes on, and disappeared, first to the bathroom and then to check on Jack. When he came back, he looked slightly nonplussed.

Danny sat up. He needed to talk to Jack about Finn's sleepwalking, but until he found the right moment, he had to use his own dubious judgment to gauge Finn's state of mind. He held out his hand. Finn took it and let Danny tug him down until he was pretty much lying on top of him. "How's Jack?"

"Right as rain."

Finn mumbled the words into Danny's chest like it was the worst news in the world. Danny frowned and nudged Finn until he had his attention. "Why's that a bad thing?"

Finn sighed. "Why do you always see right through me?"

If only. "It's your eyes. They give you away when you've got the hump." Danny ruffled Finn's hair to lighten the mood, but Finn's frown remained. "Seriously. What's up?"

"You won't get it."

"So? Doesn't mean you can't say it."

Finn chewed on his lip. He was a rugged guy, but like this —half-uncertain, half-belligerent—he looked almost boyish. "When Jack's pills kick in they knock him out for a while, then he wakes up, good as new, like it never happened."

He's not sure it really happened. Finn had told Danny before that paranoia and second-guessing himself was something he lived with every day. He opened his mouth to offer some tenuous comfort, but Finn cut him off.

"When do you have to leave?"

The blunt question caught Danny off guard. The investigation felt like a ten-ton weight on his shoulders, but without access to the case files and firm orders from the DCI to rest up, for once he didn't actually need to be anywhere else. And there was nowhere else he wanted to be either. "I'm not leaving."

Finn's expression brightened like a ray of hazy sunlight. "You don't have to work?"

"Not today."

"That's awesome." Finn scrambled off the bed and shut the door. He fiddled with the expensive, unobtrusive sound system in the corner, wriggled out of his undone jeans, and crawled back under the covers.

The quiet tones of Portishead filtered into the somewhat eerie early morning. Danny pulled Finn close and kissed the top of his head. He wanted to ask Finn again if he was okay, but he didn't. What good would it do? Finn had answered the question… twice, and Danny was still none the wiser.

They lay in a peaceful silence for a while. Finn dozed while Danny played with his hair and tried to let his steady heartbeat calm his racing mind. Murder. Schizophrenia. Murder. Schizophrenia. Whichever way Danny turned, it wasn't pretty, and for once the lure of Finn—sleepy, smiling, and beautiful—wasn't enough to distract him.

If Finn noticed Danny's preoccupation, he didn't say. When he deemed himself awake, he reached for his guitar and picked out gentle chords and riffs, Danny's idea of heaven until a phone call disturbed their quiet morning.

As had become habit of late, Danny jumped a mile and sat bolt upright. He searched out his phone where it lay dormant on the bedside table, and frowned. The screen was blank.

Finn shot him a strange look and reached over Danny to answer his own phone.

"Hi, Mum. You all right?"

Danny breathed a sigh of relief and flopped back down, ignoring Finn's continuing, curious stare, though he could well understand it. Finn's ringtone was the Ramones and nothing like the boring utilitarian beep of Danny's phone. *Dickhead.* Still, running on empty, Danny wasn't sure he could handle news of another dead girl, and listening to Finn chat shit with his mother was oddly soothing. That is until their conversation turned to Finn's health.

"I'm all right, Mum. Honest," Finn said. "Just been gigging a lot, that's all. Yeah, yeah, I know."

Finn rolled his eyes, and Danny found a grin from somewhere and plastered it on his face. Finn's relationship with his mother bemused Danny. They seemed to talk every couple of days while Danny could go weeks without a word from his own.

"Do you want to come to my mum's with me on Boxing Day?"

"Whaa?" Danny blinked, caught drifting along in that gray place between asleep and awake. When had Finn hung up the phone and dropped onto his chest. "What?"

Finn eyed him, amused. "You're away with the fairies today. I said, do you want to come to my mum's with me on Boxing Day?"

"I have to work."

Finn's face fell. It was brief but Danny saw it all the same. "Fair enough. I've got a gig on Christmas Eve at the city festival. Do you want to do something after?"

"Sure." It felt like a hollow promise, though Danny couldn't say why. He put his arms around Finn and held him close a moment, grounding himself in Finn's familiar warmth. "Sounds good."

Finn nipped Danny's chest, then sat up. "I'm hungry."

"You're always hungry." In fact Danny was surprised Finn

had lasted so long without mentioning food. "Bet your cupboards are bare, though, right?"

Finn shrugged. "Probably. No one's been home all week."

"Do you want me to go out and get something?"

Leaving Finn's bed was the last thing Danny wanted to do, but beneath the fatigue of the past few days, he was pretty hungry himself.

"Actually," Finn said, "do you fancy going *out* out, like to the greasy spoon down the road?"

That caught Danny off guard considering Finn's reaction to the supermarket the night before. "You want to go out?"

"No. I want to hide under my duvet for a week, and I'll do it if I don't go out today."

The logic made sense, but Finn's matter-of-fact tone got under Danny's skin. What kind of life was it when such simple things terrified him? Surely Finn deserved more—

Finn's kiss cut Danny's thoughts short, a softly insistent kiss that reminded Danny he'd never answered Finn's question. Not that it seemed to matter as Finn ground into him and replaced the hollow rumble in Danny's belly with an entirely different hunger.

Danny got lost in Finn's embrace, in his silky hair and rough, stubbled jaw. Finn was a lean bloke, all long legs and arms, but his frame was hard and wiry and dug into Danny in all the right places.

Finn rolled them, once, twice, and tugged at Danny's T-shirt. "Off."

As if Danny could refuse. He lost his shirt and hooked Finn in place with his legs. Finn pressed his cock against him, and Danny arched his back, welcoming the shift in their usual roles. Danny had always topped Finn—and loved it—but a part of him remained that craved the unknown sensation of Finn driving inside him.

Danny rolled them again and straddled Finn, not breaking the slow, rolling rhythm that had set them both on fire. "Feels good like this."

Finn closed his eyes. "Fuck yeah. So good. We're all right, you and me. Aren't we?"

We're all right, aren't we?

Danny froze. Finn had muttered the phrase over and over the night before, but it hadn't been until Finn was falling asleep that Danny had really heard the distress lacing every word, and by then, it was too late. Danny had fucked up, literally. An image of Finn fumbling blindly with the window catch flashed into his mind, and the heat between them morphed into a vortex that sucked the life out of every place his skin touched Finn's.

Finn sensed the shift and opened his eyes. "What's wrong?"

"Nothing." Danny pulled back. He couldn't explain it, but something felt off. He couldn't do… *that* with Finn right now.

He rolled away. Finn started to follow him, but then he stopped and sat up. "Fuck. I know what this is."

"It's not anything." Danny sat up too and looked around for his clothes. "I'm just tired, mate. That's all."

"Too tired to fuck? Or just tired of me?"

The bitterness in Finn's tone forced Danny to look at him. "Tired of you? Why would you think that?"

"Oh, come on." Finn laughed without humor. "Do you think I'm stupid as well as mental? I know I lost my shit last night. It's written all over your fucking face." He scrambled out of bed and dressed before Danny could blink. "You wouldn't be the first bloke who couldn't handle it. Just do me a favor…. Next time don't bother fucking me before you run screaming for the bloody hills."

"What? Who's screaming?"

"Can't you hear it?" Finn tapped the side of his head. "Ooh, maybe it's just me. What do you think, Danny? Does psycho look good on me? Or is it the worst thing you've ever fucking seen."

Danny didn't know what to say. Finn's anger had come from nowhere, triggered by something Danny didn't understand, but his accusation hit dangerously close to the mark. Finn's condition didn't turn Danny off, but there was no doubt in Danny's mind he'd gotten it wrong the night before. Finn hadn't needed a fuck—he'd needed a friend, and somewhere in the last twelve hours, Danny had forgotten how to be both.

"Finn…." Danny reached out, but it was too late. He'd waited too long and the damage was done.

Finn lurched away and stormed out of the room. A few minutes later, the front door slammed. The dull thud felt like a kick to Danny's chest. It was a few moments before he noticed Jack in the doorway.

"What was that all about?"

Danny retrieved his T-shirt and pulled it over his head. "Bad night."

"For him or for you?"

"Both." Danny got up and yanked his jeans on. Jack watched him through hooded eyes. Despite Finn's claims to the contrary, he looked like shit. "The supermarket thing upset him, and I didn't handle it right."

"There is no right way to handle it, Danny. You just have to be there for him."

Danny blew out a breath. Jack had said that before. *You can't just say you're going to be there for him. You've got to bloody do it.* But could he? Last night had been a test… his first real grapple with Finn's illness, and he'd failed miserably. "Is it normal for him to sleepwalk?"

"In what context?"

"Context? He got up in the night and tried to jump out the window."

Jack ventured farther into the room and sat on Finn's bed. "Yeah, he does that sometimes. Drives Will fucking crazy."

"This isn't a joke."

"I'm not laughing, but honest, mate, it's nothing to worry about. He sleepwalks when he's anxious, not when he's relapsing. If he's slipping into something, he tends not to sleep at all."

Right. Danny felt his patience evaporate. "So if I shouldn't worry about that, what *should* I worry about?"

"This." Jack pointed at Finn's open bedroom door. "Finn's the nicest guy in the world. He only yells at people when he's shitting a brick. You need to figure out what's bugging him and fix it."

"Fix it?"

"Or at least convince him it's okay to be scared. Finn worries about stuff you and me don't even notice. He's likely got himself worked up over something really bloody stupid."

Danny wasn't so sure, but he didn't feel like explaining to Jack how he'd pulled away from Finn in a moment Finn had probably needed him more than ever. Instead he settled for, "It wasn't his fault. I've got a lot on at work and I haven't been around much. I wasn't paying attention and I fucked up."

Jack was silent a moment, then he seemed to make a decision. "Finn's been well for a long time. The last time he lost it was because someone fucked him over."

"A boyfriend?"

"Yeah. Finn got agitated over something small and the bloke he was with freaked… made more of it than it was, and pushed him over the edge."

"Into an episode?"

Jack grimaced. "Yep. And he didn't hang around to fix the damage either. He was long gone by the time Finn was well enough to see anyone, and that shit stayed with Finn… still does. You're the first bloke he's brought home in years."

Danny filed the information away in his already overloaded brain. He'd known from the beginning that being with Finn would be challenging, but he felt sorely unprepared for the way Jack was looking at him now… like Danny held all the answers, when he'd never felt so fucking out of his depth. "I don't know where he's gone."

"Not far." Jack got up and drifted to the door. "If I know Finn, he's probably smoking my fags in the park. He'll be back soon enough. If I was you, mate, I'd sit tight and put the kettle on."

Danny sighed as Jack mooched back to wherever he'd come from. A cup of tea sounded like the best idea in the world, but without Finn to overpour the milk and flick sugar in his hair, nothing felt right.

CHAPTER ELEVEN

FINN TEXTED him later: *I'm sorry.*

No need. My fault, Danny shot back.

Nope. Definitely mine.

Are you okay?

Yep. Saw my nurse. Got my jab. I'm good.

Then so am I.

Call you later?

Anytime.

"*THE SLEEPY Stargazer,* eh? Mate, you're such a contradiction."

Finn ignored Bigsy's gentle ribbing and concentrated on the nativity unfolding on the tiny stage of the local church school. The hall was packed with parents and community figures, but for once Finn didn't mind the crowd. Watching the children perform the songs he'd pretty much rewritten was oddly fascinating, and not even Bigsy taking the piss could distract him.

Shame Bigsy didn't care. "Are you coming over after? We're gonna get a curry in."

Finn wanted to refuse. He'd felt antisocial all week, but it was a few days before Christmas Eve, and he hadn't seen Bigsy's kids in ages.

"Bring Danny if you want."

Christ. Did it ever stop? "Danny's working," Finn muttered. And it was true. Danny had worked nonstop since Finn's embarrassing temper tantrum, and despite a few text assurances to the contrary, Finn was starting to worry he'd fucked things up for good.

The lack of resolution bugged him. Danny had been long gone by the time Finn had simmered down enough to go home. Jack said he'd been called into work, but Finn wasn't convinced.

Serves you right for having a hissy fit. Heat flooded Finn's cheeks for all the wrong reasons. His last encounter with Danny had been a clusterfuck from the start. Only the sex made sense—at least it had until Danny had made it clear it wasn't something he wanted to repeat in a hurry.

"It's not that, Finn. I just feel like we should've talked more before we got down and dirty. We can't use sex as a distraction when things get tough."

Danny's logic—conveyed over a snatched phone call—made sense, but Finn didn't like it. Danny seemed like a man with the weight of the world on his shoulders. What if Finn's burden became too much for them both?

The final song of the nativity roused Finn from his brooding. He smiled. The original track had been the tackiest of the lot, and Finn had spent long hours reworking it into something that fit the beautiful set and costumes Ben's sister had designed. All things considered, it had come out pretty well. Finn had even caught Danny whistling it in the shower.

Danny. Fuck's sake.

The concert drew to a close. Bigsy punched Finn's arm. "Well done, mate. Much better than the utter shit I sat through at Emily's school yesterday."

Finn laughed. "Better than the aliens in Bethlehem? I don't believe that."

"You will. Karen videoed it. Come on. Let's pick up some grub and head back to mine."

Bigsy's tone left no room for argument, and Finn let himself be hustled into Ben's car and driven across town to the overcrowded terraced house Bigsy and his family called home. On the way they picked up enough Indian food to feed a small army. Bigsy's kids ran out to meet them. Finn heaved a toddler onto his shoulders and felt halfway human for the first time in more than a week.

A rowdy dinner followed. The kids went to bed and the adults kicked back, crammed around Bigsy's kitchen table, and reminisced about years gone by. For the most part, Finn just listened. He'd had his share of wild nights out, but he had nothing on Bigsy and Jack when they were left unsupervised.

Bigsy left the table and disappeared into the garage. He came back dressed as Batman and struck a pose, pointing a beer bottle at Jack. "Face it, mate. I'm a superhero."

Karen snorted in a way that belied her delicate frame. "Dickhead, more like. Whatever happened to your Robin suit, Jack? Because I know you didn't take it back to Germany."

"Your *what*?" Will raised an eyebrow. "When did this happen? Why haven't I seen this?"

Jack's face was the picture of innocence. "I don't know what she's talking about."

"Bollocks." Finn kicked Jack under the table. "It's in the loft. I saw it when I got the Christmas decs down."

"Shut *up*."

Karen cackled and snaked an arm around Will's slim shoulders. "Bigsy and Jack went to that beer festival in Berlin a few summers ago. I think you were doing exams or something. I don't know what the hell they drank, but they got off the plane dressed as bloody Batman and Robin."

Bigsy had the good grace to look sheepish. He returned to

his seat beside Karen and jerked his head at Jack. "It was his idea."

"Prove it," Jack shot back. "I don't remember a thing. We didn't even know where we got the costumes from until Finn found the shop receipt under his pillow."

"Yeah, and I still don't know what you were doing in my bed." Finn swiped the last of Jack's naan bread. He fancied a beer, but he'd had too many dodgy days of late to risk it. "I woke up to find you both on top of me."

"Daft idiots. You were supposed to fly into Gatwick, not Leeds. You missed my parents' golden wedding anniversary." Karen leaned over and whacked Bigsy upside his head.

Bigsy fell off his chair. Finn laughed so hard his ribs ached. As a band they'd had a busy few months, and he'd missed this—spending time with his mates without the pressure of live shows or studio time. The only thing missing was, as ever, Danny, but with a full belly and the warmth of his pseudo-family around him, Finn found it in him to feel hopeful. Danny had promised over and over that the schizophrenia and the bullshit that came with it wouldn't drive him away. Perhaps it was time Finn believed him.

The doorbell cut through the raucous laughter. Bigsy hauled himself from the floor to answer it. Finn followed him, heading for the bathroom. He had his hand on the door when Bigsy's exclamation stopped him in his tracks.

"Danny? What's up, mate? Everything all right?"

Finn spun around, sure he'd misheard, but sure enough there was Danny, standing on Bigsy's doorstep, his face graver than Finn had ever seen.

Bigsy took a step back. He jerked his head in Finn's direction. "Come on in. Finn's around here somewhere."

Danny shook his head and flashed his ID. "I'm not here for Finn, Bigsy. I'm working. You're Darren Biggs, right?"

Bigsy opened his mouth. Shut it again. "Er, yeah. Shit. I didn't know you were a copper."

"Vice squad," Danny said. "Can we come in? I need to talk to you about your sister."

Fuck. For the first time, Finn noticed the flashing lights of a police car and the uniformed officers hovering at Danny's back. What the hell had Gemma done now? That girl was going to send what remained of Bigsy's family into an early grave.

Danny stepped into the house. He met Finn's gaze, briefly, but his expression was unreadable. "Bigsy, where's your missus, mate?"

"In the kitchen… I…."

"I'll get her." Finn shot back to the kitchen and grabbed Karen. The others shot him puzzled looks. "Stay in here," he said. "The rozzers are here about Gemma."

Finn escorted Karen to the living room, where Danny and a female police officer had shepherded Bigsy. He started to back away and shut the door behind him.

Bigsy caught his arm. "Stay. This is bad. I can feel it."

Finn patted Bigsy's shoulder. He wanted to say something encouraging, but he could feel in his own bones that Bigsy was right.

Danny cleared his throat. "I'm going to call you Bigsy, because that's how I know you. That okay?"

Bigsy shrugged. "Fine by me. What's going on, mate? Is Gemma in trouble?"

"First, can you confirm that Gemma Louise Biggs is your sister?"

"Yeah, yeah. That's her. What's she done?"

Danny paused, and perhaps Finn was the only one in the room who noticed the brief slip in his composure. "I'm sorry to have to inform you Gemma was found dead last night."

Silence. Finn was sure his own heart had stopped.

Bigsy swallowed. "What?"

"She's dead," Danny said. "A maintenance worker found her body by Junction 25 of the M1."

"Fuck." Bigsy paled. Karen squeezed his hand and for a moment he was gone... lost. "How did she die? Was it the drugs?"

"You knew she was using?" Danny caught the gaze of the female officer beside him.

Bigsy nodded. "Yeah. She's been on junk since she was fifteen."

"And she was eighteen?"

"Was?" Bigsy shook his head. "Fuck me. Was. I can't believe this shit."

Danny gave him a minute, looking anywhere but at Finn, then seemed to steel himself. "Were you aware that Gemma was working as a prostitute?"

Karen gasped and clapped her hands over her mouth, but Bigsy just stared... stared hard at Danny, like he could force him to take the words back. "She wouldn't do that."

Danny leaned forward. "I'm sorry, mate. I saw her myself. She was living in a squat down Becker Road and calling herself Jade."

"Jade? What the fuck? That's our dog's name." Bigsy put his head in his hands, and for a long moment, nobody spoke. A clock ticked on the mantelpiece like the menacing beat of an enemy drum, and Finn felt like the world would surely implode and swallow them all up.

"Oh God." Bigsy sat up. "You found her by the motorway. Fuck, fuck, fuck. How did she die? Was it him? Did he get her?"

The words meant nothing to Finn, but in that moment, he knew they meant everything to Danny.

"We don't know anything for sure right now," Danny said. "I need you to ignore what you've seen in the media and wait for the postmortem."

"Bollocks." Bigsy stood, shoving Karen off him like a ragdoll. "You already know, don't you? That sick fuck serial killer has murdered my sister."

Finn's heart dropped through the floor. He took a breath that lodged in his throat and wouldn't budge. Danny glanced at him like he knew, and Finn's hands twitched. He looked away. *Get a grip, dammit. This isn't about you.*

Danny got up and walked to the window where Bigsy had drifted. He spoke in a voice low enough for only Bigsy to hear. Finn crouched by the sofa and put his hand on Karen's knee. "You okay?"

Karen blew out a breath. "Bloody hell. That girl was always going to die young, but this?" She shook her head. "She deserved better than this. They all did."

Finn didn't know what to say. Bigsy's family had been through hell three times over with the loss of first their father in the Falklands, then their mother a few years back. Gemma had been in trouble for years and the ending had always seemed inevitable, but now it was here it felt so fucking cruel.

Bigsy appeared beside them. He looked a little calmer, though his ashen skin gave him away. "I need to go with the coppers and formally identify the body."

"I'll go with you," Karen said.

"No. I'll be all right, love. I need to do this by myself."

"You should get changed, at least." Karen touched the Batman costume. "Come on. I'll get your jeans out of the dryer."

Karen pulled a dazed Bigsy from the room. It took Finn a few moments to realize he was alone with Danny in perhaps the strangest circumstances he could ever imagine.

Danny grasped Finn's shoulder and pulled him to his feet. "You okay?"

"Me? God. This is crazy. Is this…. Gemma? Is she your case?"

"One of them."

"How many others?"

"Gemma was the fourth."

"I had no idea. I mean… I saw something on the news last

week, but I never thought...." Finn stopped. "Is this why you've been so distracted?"

"I'd imagine so." Danny tried a smile. Failed. "I'm sorry I didn't tell you, I just—"

"It's okay," Finn said. "I should've figured there was more going on than the shit in my own head."

Danny gripped Finn's arm. "Don't do that. I've told you already, a thousand times, none of that is gonna drive me away, okay? I just need to deal with this. People are getting killed on my watch. I can't do anything until we've caught the bastard."

"You need to catch him, Danny. Bigsy will lose his bloody mind if you don't. He's been through enough."

"Did you know her?"

"Gemma? No, not really. She's always been around, but she's... she was like a ghost, you know? Thinner and paler every time I saw her."

"How often did you see her?"

Finn raised an eyebrow. "Are you asking officially?"

"Not yet, but anything you can tell me will help and give me less reason to hassle Bigsy."

That was good enough for Finn. "Gemma's been trouble since Bigsy's parents died."

"Their mother died a few years ago?"

"Right. Six... maybe seven years ago. Breast cancer. Gemma went off the rails pretty soon after. She ran off with some no-good bloke when she was fifteen. She never really came back."

Danny nodded. Finn could see him adding it all to what Bigsy had already told him and coming up with a picture too awful for Finn to comprehend.

"She wasn't always a mess, though. I met her when she was fourteen, and she was probably the most beautiful girl I'd ever seen."

Danny smiled sadly. "I saw her a few weeks ago, and she was still beautiful. Listen. I've got to go. Are you okay?"

"Me? Shit. Yeah. I'm all right. It's just a shock. I can't, fuck…. Bigsy. I can't imagine how he's feeling."

"I know." Danny released Finn's arm and started to turn away.

Finn stopped him. "Danny?"

"Yeah?"

Please don't go. "Be careful out there."

CHAPTER TWELVE

LOUD, INSISTENT banging woke Danny from his uncomfortable sleep on the couch. He rolled off and hit the floor with a dull thud. Shit. He'd passed out in his clothes. The banging came again. He scrambled to his feet, shucked his coat, and started for the front door. On the way he tripped over the bag of take-away food he'd forgotten to eat. Cold kebab, anyone?

Nice.

Danny threw open his front door. His old mate Kev glared back at him.

"Finally. Don't you answer your bloody phone anymore?"

"What?" Danny looked around for his phone. Recently it had seemed glued to his ear. "When did you call me?"

"I've been calling you all feckin' morning. You have a visitor at my place. Seems you forgot to tell your baby sister you moved."

Danny flicked his gaze rapidly between Kev and his phone screen, unsure he'd heard him right, but the six missed calls from Kev was a bit of a giveaway. "Sara's in Nottingham?"

"Yep. Spent the night in your old room. Where the fuck have you been?"

"Working." Danny rubbed his face and looked around for something, anything, to wake him up.

"On the serial-killer thing?"

"What do you think?"

Kev grunted. "Figured as much. Haven't seen you around lately."

Danny let that one go. "What's Sara doing here? Why didn't she call me?"

"I don't bloody know. She didn't seem too happy to find you'd moved out, though. Why didn't you tell her?"

"I did. At least I told my mum." And then it clicked into place. Danny's mother had always disparaged the pedestal Danny's younger sister had put him on, and with more than a decade between the two siblings, it hadn't been hard to push them apart. Danny hadn't seen Sara in months, and even then it had been a snatched cup of coffee in Leeds. "Is she still at your place?"

"No, she's in the car. Figured I'd check you were decent before I sent her up."

Danny glared, though given the state of his neglected flat, he was glad Kev had been so considerate. He chucked his abandoned dinner in the bin. "I'd better go down and get her."

"Don't bother," Kev said. "Jump in the shower. I'll send her up."

Danny did just that. He turned the water as hot as he dared and tried to calm his exploding brain. He was halfway through another twenty-four-hour mandatory downtime, but in reality he'd worked every hour he'd been awake since he'd discovered the true identity of the fourth girl. He hadn't had the balls to tell Bigsy his sister had been snatched from the streets right under his nose, but fuck, Danny couldn't get it out of his head. He'd known Gemma was at risk the moment he'd laid eyes on her, and he'd left her out there. Left her to die, and lie, undiscovered, for more than a week.

Stop it.

Jen Lanes's voice cut through the chaos. Danny had spent a long afternoon with her researching convicted offenders in the local area, particularly those with a history of violence against women, and, as ever, she'd proved the voice of reason.

Every girl out there is at risk. All we can do is catch the bastard.

And bloody hell, they'd tried. Together they'd scrutinized each victim and scene over and over. Made notes of the patterns and anomalies and circled the subtle signs the killer was becoming more careless... reckless, until it almost felt like the killer *wanted* to be caught and they were just too stupid to catch him.

"Danny! Get your fucking arse out here."

Danny shut the shower off, dried, and tied a towel around his waist. The indignant face of his beautiful younger sister greeted him when he opened the bathroom door, and he blinked. Saw Jade... Gemma's face, like he had done so often since he'd been called to her rudimentary grave.

"Earth to Danny?"

Danny forced a grin and pushed past Sara's slender frame. "Yeah, yeah. What the fuck are you doing here?"

"Nice. Do you kiss all the boys with that mouth?"

Danny threw a startled glance over his shoulder. As a rule, blood relatives never mentioned his sexuality. He grabbed some clothes from the wardrobe and absently pulled them on. Scruffy jeans. Finn's Stone Roses T-shirt. How had that ended up here? "Do Mum and Dad know where you are?"

"They do, actually. Mum rang me, ranting that you'd stopped answering her e-mails. I told her you were busy and we were spending Christmas together up here, so technically I'm here to protect you."

Christmas. Fuck. It was bloody Christmas Eve and Danny hadn't even noticed. "I never answer Mum's e-mails. They go to my junk box."

"Harsh."

Danny shrugged. "She knows where to find me if it matters."

And it never did. It never had.

"So… can I?"

"Hmm?" Danny came out of his room to find Sara slumped on his couch, feet up on the coffee table. "Can you what?"

"Spend Christmas with you."

"Sis, I'm working all week."

"I know, but I can just hang around here, can't I? You have to come home sometimes, Danny. Please? I don't want to go home and watch her make Dad miserable."

Danny sighed. How could he refuse? He hadn't spent Christmas at home in years for that very reason. "You'll be bored."

"Won't."

"You will."

"When are you working today?"

She had him there. Barring any significant developments Danny wasn't due back until dawn the following morning. "I'm off."

Sara's face brightened, and for a moment, though they were like night and day, her sunny smile reminded him of Finn. "Can we go shopping?"

Or maybe not. Danny couldn't imagine those four evil words ever coming out of Finn's mouth. "Shopping? Really?"

"Unless you've already bought my present?"

Oops. Christmas tended to pass Danny by, and the best Sara usually got was fifty quid in a card in January. Unbidden Danny's mind flashed back to Bigsy's house, all lit up with life and laughter. Danny had conducted more death notifications than he cared to remember, and Bigsy's reaction had been muted given the horrific circumstances of his sister's death, but watching that cloud descend over Bigsy's vibrant family would stay with him forever.

"*Danny!*"

"All right, all right. I'm coming."

They left Danny's flat and drove into the city to do battle with the crowds of last-minute shoppers. Sara hustled Danny straight into Punkyfish and held up a dress held together with rubber and string.

"What do you think?"

Danny glared. "No"

Sara put the dress back. "What about this?"

"No."

"This?"

"Are you taking the piss?"

"Finally… he gives a shit." Sara rolled her eyes and drifted to another rail.

Danny trailed after her. "I give a shit."

"Right. So what have you been up to?"

"Working, the usual. What's with all the PVC crap?"

Sara eyed Danny over an item of clothing Danny couldn't even identify. "I'm going to a goth night on New Year's Eve. I need something vampy."

"Vampy, not trampy." Danny pried the hanger from Sara's hands. "If I take you to River Island, will you pick something that doesn't look like a melted bin bag?"

"Are you paying?"

"Fifty quid." Danny pointed at the door. "Let's go."

MUCH, *MUCH* later and seventy quid lighter, Danny took Sara to the pub for lunch. Student life had left her slimmer and paler than he was used to, and though he felt like the worst big brother in the world, buying her a plate of pie and chips was easy. Shame having a conversation was anything but.

"So what would you be doing if I hadn't turned up on your doorstep?"

Danny shrugged, still not altogether sure why Sara had shown up in Nottingham when she should've been at their family home in Cardiff. "It wasn't my doorstep. It was Kev's."

"How was I supposed to know that?"

"You want to row about that again?"

"No." Sara's tone turned sullen. She pushed her remaining food around her plate, and Danny took a moment to remind himself of the twelve years between them. Their parents had Danny's address, but Sara was eighteen and wrapped up in her first year at uni. Besides, it wasn't like he'd even thought to tell Sara he'd moved.

Danny took a breath to apologize, but Sara spoke first.

"Why are you always like this?"

"Like what?"

"So bloody vague when I take an interest in your life?"

"I'm not vague."

"Yes, you are." Sara pushed her plate away. "I ask where you've been, you say 'nowhere.' I ask what you've been doing, you say 'nothing,' and when I ask who you've been seeing, you say 'no one.' What the fuck, Danny? Is there nothing in your life you want to tell me about?"

"Tell you about? What do you want me to say? I'm an adult. I have a job, and when I'm not working, I'm doing boring shit like paying bills and getting my car serviced. There's nothing to tell."

"Bollocks. You just don't give a shit, do you? Well, you know what? Fuck you. If you're not bothered, neither am I."

Sara shoved her chair back and stormed out of the café. Danny rolled his eyes, knowing he'd find her sniffling on the bench outside. Sara had always had a temper. Danny remembered studying for his GCSE exams with her slamming her Barbie doll beach set into his bedroom wall, enraged at being sent to bed early for throwing a plate at their mother. In hindsight she'd had a point, but life had moved on… hadn't it?

He paid the bill and drifted outside. Sara met his gaze with red-rimmed eyes.

"Are you really happy here, Danny? Or did you come here just to hide from Mum?"

Danny didn't know what to say. He *hadn't* been happy in Nottingham until he'd met Finn, but he hadn't realized the depth of his loneliness either. And how did he explain that to his baby sister? A girl, in truth, he hardly knew. "What do you want from me?"

"I want you to tell me about your life." Sara stopped, eyes shining with those stubborn tears she'd never let fall, even as the tiny toddler Danny still remembered her being. "I just want to know you."

"I—" Danny's phone cut him off. He pulled it out of his pocket and eyed the screen with a healthy amount of trepidation, but it wasn't work—it was Finn.

Thinking of you.

Danny sighed. He knew the scene at Bigsy's house had hurt Finn, scared him, and it cut Danny deeply that he hadn't been able to put his arms around Finn and tell him he wouldn't rest until Gemma's killer had been caught. For the past few days, sporadic texts had been all they'd had.

"Who's that?"

"Hmm?" Danny looked up, startled to be caught staring at his phone, half forgetting he'd pushed his baby sister so far away she was screaming in the street to get him to hear her.

I just want to know you. Her words haunted him. He couldn't tell her even half of what was going on in his life, but Finn was playing a gig a few streets away, headlining Nottingham's biggest winter festival with just his guitar and his shy grin. He could tell her that, couldn't he? "Come on. I'll show you."

They walked to the city center Christmas carnival. By Finn's standards the gig was low-key, but the streets were rammed and the queue for the free event stretched all the way down one side of the main street.

Sara eyed the posters and billboards, curious and puzzled.

"Is this the festival Noel Gallagher turned up and busked at last year?"

"Yep."

"Who have they got this year?"

Danny grinned. "No idea. Nottingham's best-kept secret."

It was true. Danny only knew Finn was playing because he was in the loop, and he'd got the feeling Finn liked it that way. The Lamps were a big deal, but Finn seemed shy about his solo work, like it was more personal... intimate... and Danny supposed it was.

They made it into the festival and grabbed a couple of beers. The sight of Sara with a pint of ale in each hand was slightly perturbing, but Danny ignored it and searched out the music tent, knowing Finn's headline acoustic set was just a few minutes away.

He spotted Finn's guitar before the man himself. Finn's beloved old Gibson was in its stand, resting beside a stool and a mic. Danny's heart quickened. He loved the Lamps and was even growing to dig Jack's eclectic dance beats, but there was something enchanting about Finn and his guitar, and judging by the teeming throng around the small stage, he wasn't the only one who thought so.

Danny found a spot to the side of the big marquee. The gig, though packed, was mellow, and the tent was strewn with cushions and beanbags. He guided Sara to a cozy area and pushed her down. "Sit."

Sara sat. "You're being very mysterious."

"No, I'm not. There's someone I want you to meet after the show."

"*After* the show?" Sara craned her neck to see the stage just as the lights dimmed. "Why after... are they coming to watch—oh my God, is that the singer from the Lamps? Bloody hell. I *love* their stuff."

"You do?" Last Danny knew Sara had been dancing around her room to Justin Timberlake. "Who else do you like?"

Sara ignored him and rose up on her knees to get a better look at the stage. "This is so awesome. They played the corn exchange in Leeds in fresher's week. I had to blag the cash from Dad to go, but it was so worth it. They smashed it."

Danny did a quick calculation in his head. Fresher's week would've been back in September, and he hadn't met Finn until late October. Not that it mattered. It just felt a little odd to know Sara had seen Finn in the flesh before he had. "They play the Hayloft here every few months or so. Finn lives in Nottingham."

"Finn?" Sara shot him a wide-eyed glance. "You mean, Finn McGovern? You know him?"

"A little. We're, uh, kind of together." Danny struggled to contain his smirk. It felt strange to be talking about Finn with anyone outside of Finn's close-knit circle, let alone Sara, but at the same time, it felt... good—liberating, in a way—and he suddenly found he could breathe a little easier.

Sara's megawatt grin and squeal of excitement helped. "He's your boyfriend?"

"Erm." Boyfriend. Danny had avoided the term since his last relationship had ended on an unpleasantly damp squib, but as the stage lit up and he met Finn's surprised gaze head-on, despite all the shadow of death and heartache around them, everything felt right. "Yeah... yeah, that's him."

Finn's forty-five-minute set flew by in a blur. Danny found himself, as ever, hypnotized by Finn's melancholy jam, and it seemed like no time at all had passed before Finn wrapped up his Nina Simone encore and dropped discreetly onto the cushion beside him with a curious, tentative smile.

"You brought a friend?"

Danny grinned. He felt oddly relaxed, given the weight of the investigation hanging over him. "This is my sister, Sara."

"Your sister? Wow, but she's so much prettier than you."

Finn reached for Sara and pulled her into a hug. She was glowing when he let her go.

"I've never met any of Danny's boyfriends before," she said.

Something changed in Finn, shifted... opened, and his grin widened enough to make Danny feel warm all over. "You live in Leeds, right? So we can crash with you next time we play the union?"

"The Lamps are going to play at the union?"

"I'd imagine so. We did last year."

"How did I not know this?" Sara clambered across Danny and inserted herself neatly between them.

Danny rolled his eyes, but on the inside it felt like yet another aspect of his personal life was clicking unexpectedly into place. He sat back and watched them talk for a while. Finn was buzzing from his gig, the agitation that often plagued him absent, and at his best no one could resist his charm, least of all Sara.

Danny let his mind drift. Sara's appearance had caught him off guard and yanked him back into a reality that had been all but obliterated by the ongoing murder investigation. He hardly knew the spunky young woman, so deep in conversation with the man he was growing to love, but watching Sara with Finn, it felt like she'd always been there... like they both had. So why did Danny feel such a heavy sense of foreboding?

Danny's phone vibrated in his pocket. He jumped on it before its pealing ring could disturb the serene postgig glow of the music tent. "Lanes?"

"Can you talk?"

"Hang on." Danny caught Finn's gaze and scrambled to his feet. He stepped over the sea of bodies lounging around the tent and made for the exit, pushing through the crowd until he found a quiet spot. "What is it?"

"The DNA results came back."

"And?" They'd been waiting on the results from the fourth crime scene—the layby where Gemma Biggs's body had been dumped—for a couple of days. The other scenes had turned up little of any use, but the forensic team had been more hopeful of the fourth.

"I've found a match in the system. We've got him, Danny. We've fucking got him."

Danny's blood ran cold. "I'm on my way."

He hung up and pushed his way back into the tent. Finn read him in an instant.

"You need to go?"

"Yeah. Sara, get your shit together. I need to drop you at Kev's on my way."

Sara frowned. "What? But—"

"She can stay with me," Finn said. "I'll take her back to the house with the boys."

Danny held Finn's gaze. He didn't have time to negotiate, but in that moment, something stopped him from running out on Finn without pulling him close and whispering, "Take care of her."

Finn squeezed Danny in a death grip. "I will, Danny. I promise. Just do what you need to do and come back to us."

CHAPTER THIRTEEN

DANNY DASHED across the city and made it to the station just as the DCI was gearing up to launch a raid.

Lanes passed Danny the suspect's file. "Take a look at this shit."

The buzz of the department faded away. Danny sank into the DCI's chair and got his first look at the monster they'd been chasing all these weeks: Bill Hughes, a nomadic lorry mechanic from Liverpool with a long history of petty crime. His DNA was on file from a fencing charge ten years ago. On the surface he looked fairly innocuous. Without the decade-old conviction, they'd never have noticed him. "Fuck. It's him, isn't it?"

Lanes met his gaze with haunted eyes. "I think so. He doesn't look the type, but this feels...."

She didn't have to finish. Danny knew, and as he looked around at the band of officers gathered for the swoop, he realized they all did. Royal fuckups notwithstanding, they had their man.

After an update from Lanes and the DCI, Danny assembled the raiding team. As the lead detective on the case, this was his show. He tooled up—stab vest, Taser, cuffs—and swapped his coat for a police-issue jacket. It had been a few months since he'd been on a major sting, and he'd never led an operation quite like this.

The DCI opened the final briefing. After he'd said his piece, he passed the reins to Danny.

Danny pinned the suspect's photo to the ops board. "Bill Hughes, wanted in connection with the murders of Ruth Maddox, Donna Preston, Selina Smith, and… Gemma Biggs. We have plainclothes officers outside his address already. He's inside and it looks like he's packing up, so we need to move fast. Daniels and Hollis at the front. Jenkins and Rhodes at the back. Parker and Hills, you take the door. Lanes and I will secure the suspect. Uniform as backup. Any questions?"

None were forthcoming. Danny knocked his fist on the suspect's grainy face. "Let's roll."

They traipsed out to the cars, five vehicles in all. The suspect's address was less than a mile away, and it struck Danny as darkly ironic that they'd been hunting up and down the M1 for someone right on their doorstep.

Danny got in the passenger seat of the lead car with Lanes at his side and two uniformed officers in the back. The powerful unmarked purred to life, and Lanes pulled out of the station car park. The drive passed in a flash. Danny directed each car to block access in and out of the unassuming terraced house and counted down on the radio.

Then they hit the ground running. Officers disappeared around the back of the property, and the front door caved in with a splintering crash.

Danny hurdled the wreckage and darted through the empty hallway. The two reception rooms were clear, the kitchen too. Danny made for the stairs with Lanes hot on his heels. He heard movement ahead of him, and then a body blocked the light at the top of the stairs. Danny looked up and met the gaze of a startled middle-aged man. Balding, over-weight, faded tattoos, Bill Hughes looked like every other bloke propping up the bar at a dodgy local pub, but then something changed. Danny shouted his warning and Bill Hughes sprang to life.

Hughes charged at Danny with a low growl. The impact of the heavier man caught Danny off guard. He stumbled back into Lanes and grabbed the bannister to steady himself, but Hughes had gravity in his favor and the three of them tumbled down the stairs.

They landed in a heap. Danny grappled with the weight pinning him down. In the chaos he caught a flash of silver slicing through the empty air.

Lanes screamed, "Danny, he's got a knife!"

Danny's vision narrowed to the dangle of limbs on the grotty carpet of the dilapidated house. He yelled for backup and took an elbow to the gut. Lanes took a knee to the face and then Hughes was up and running, slashing the crude kitchen knife to keep Danny at bay.

Lanes let out a grunt of pain. Danny scrambled to his feet and reached for her. She pushed him away. "I'm okay, I'm okay. Go, go, *go*!"

Danny tore through the ground floor of the house with four officers behind him. Hughes had made for the back door, now guarded by Jenkins and Rhodes. Less than a minute had passed since Hughes had barged Danny down the stairs, but as he looked ahead and watched Hughes plunge his knife into Jenkins's neck, it felt like a lifetime.

Jenkins fell to the floor. Rhodes dropped to help him. Danny yelled for assistance and leaped over them both. Ahead of him Hughes disappeared down an alleyway the officers watching the house before the raid had failed to mention.

Danny sprinted after him. Adrenaline surged in his veins, laced with a real fear he'd find himself cornered in a dead end, just him, a blade, and serial killer. But it didn't happen. The alleyway came to an end and Hughes hit the streets.

Screams and the screech of tires reached Danny's ears. He emerged from the alleyway in time to see Hughes make a brazen dash through the busy Christmas Eve traffic, holding his bloody knife aloft.

Danny followed. Behind him he heard the shouts of the officers on his tail, and above, the first drone of the police helicopter. But Danny couldn't wait for the chopper or the panda cars wailing through the traffic to reach him. Hughes had a knife, blood on his hands, and nothing to lose.

He had his hands on Hughes when the car struck them both. Jarring pain roared from Danny's hip to his shoulder, and then his head as he landed on the pavement a few feet away with Hughes once again on top of him. Danny rolled, ignoring the crunch of bones in his left side, and pinned Hughes to the ground. Dimly he was aware of screams and heavy footfalls bearing down on them, and then blood oozing out of Hughes beneath him… and dripping down Danny's own face.

Danny jammed the cuffs on Hughes. He'd known his face for less than an hour, but the venom he felt was consuming. Hate, anger, horror; in that moment Danny felt them all.

"Bill Hughes, I'm arresting you for the murders of Ruth Maddox, Donna Preston, Selina Smith, and Gemma Biggs. You do not have to say anything, but it may harm your defense if you do not mention, when questioned, something which you later rely on in court. Anything you do say may be given in evidence."

Hughes grunted. "Fuck you. Little slags had it coming."

Danny saw red, but strong hands pulled him away before he realized he'd raised his hand. Lanes. She dragged him a few feet and crouched in front of him, her nose bleeding and set at an awkward angle.

"We've got him, Danny. Just hold on, okay? The ambulance is coming."

CHAPTER FOURTEEN

IT WAS 2:00 p.m. on Christmas Day when Danny finally called. Finn jumped on his phone before the vibration morphed into his Ramones ringtone. "Danny?"

"Please tell me you know where my sister is?"

Finn got up from the couch and slipped out of the living room, leaving most of the band, and Sara, glued to the news like they had been all night, ever since the news had filtered through about the knife-wielding serial killer roaming the city streets. He shut the door and went to the kitchen. "She's here. She's safe. She's chatting up Jack."

Danny chuckled, wry and tired. "Lucky Jack."

"Are you okay? They said on the news that maniac was running around with a sword or some shit, and a copper got stabbed. Please tell me it wasn't you?"

"It wasn't. I got hit by a car instead."

"What? Where are you? Are you all right?"

"Kind of. I'm at Queens A and E still. That's why I'm calling. Could you… could you come and get me?"

"Of course." Finn already had his keys in his hand. "Do you need me to bring anything?"

"Some clothes, maybe? I might have some lying around your place."

"No worries. I'll be twenty minutes, okay?"

"Yeah… bye."

Danny hung up and Finn stared at his phone a moment, frozen in that place where it took reality a moment to fall into place. Something as ever felt off, and then it clicked…. He'd never, ever heard Danny ask for help, for anything, from anyone, let alone Finn.

He needs me. The realization hit Finn like a brick wall, but he found himself in motion before he could dwell on it. He flew upstairs and threw clothes in a bag—his, Danny's, maybe Jack's, he wasn't sure—then dashed back down and beckoned Jack out of the living room. "Danny called. I'm going to go and pick him up. Can you look after Sara? I'll come and get her in a bit."

Jack nodded. "Danny all right?"

"I don't know," Finn said. "He's at the hospital. I'll know more when I see him."

"What about Bigsy? Have you heard from him yet?"

Finn shook his head. Bigsy had gone to ground since the media had exploded with news of the dramatic breakthrough in the murder case. "I'll go round tomorrow."

"Only if Danny doesn't need you. Otherwise I'll go over with Will. You can't look after everyone."

As if. How much time had Jack lost looking after Finn? "I'll call you when I know more."

"All right, mate."

Finn left and drove the six short miles to the hospital he knew well. The psychiatric unit was on the third floor, and even on a good day, the sight of it always made him feel a bit strange. But not today. Finn threw the van into a parking space with nothing in his mind but Danny, getting to him, putting his hands on him, and seeing with his own eyes that he was safe. Even the throngs of press and police at the hospital entrance hardly registered.

He slipped past them all, head down, face half-hidden in

his jacket, and went to the front desk. "I'm here for Danny Jones? He's a police officer."

The graying man behind the desk frowned a moment, then clicked a few buttons on his computer, and his expression became grave enough to scare the ever-loving shit out of Finn. "Wait there. I'll get someone to come and speak to you."

The man disappeared, and the wait for another soul to appear felt like a lifetime. Finn's mind raced, his stomach in his boots. Danny had called… asked Finn to pick him up, so logic told Finn his injuries couldn't be that severe, but half an hour had passed since that call. What if—

"Finn McGovern?"

Finn whipped around. A slim black woman stood behind him, her face a bruised mess. "Yeah?"

"Detective Lanes." The woman held out her hand. "Danny's just getting discharged. I'll take you to him."

Finn followed the woman through a set of double doors. "Is he okay?"

"He will be. He broke a rib. Some stitches in his head. He scared the crap out of me when I saw him covered in blood, but it could've been a lot worse."

Finn knew that—God, he knew that—but it still felt like the worst thing in the world. "How did it happen?"

The detective snorted. "He jumped in front of a car to save the world. Typical bloody Danny."

Was it? Finn had no idea, and as he looked beyond the woman and caught his first glimpse of Danny sitting shirtless on a bed in blood-soaked jeans, covered in bruises, he didn't much care.

"Danny?"

Danny looked up, startled, like he'd been somewhere else entirely. He didn't say anything, just held out his hand, but for Finn the gesture said everything. He took Danny's hand and moved close enough for Danny to lean on him.

"All right? They said you broke a rib," Finn said.

"Yep."

"And your head?" Finn put two fingers under Danny's chin and inspected the damage. A one-inch gash was hidden just beyond Danny's hairline, and the source, no doubt, of the dried blood flaking from behind his ear. "That looks nasty."

"Scalp wounds bleed a lot."

Finn eyed the blood staining Danny's jeans. "I'll say. I brought you some clean clothes. Here, I'll help you."

Finn pulled the curtain around the bed and helped Danny into a clean set of clothes while Danny remained dazed and silent, like he could drop off the earth at any moment. Finn touched his cheek.

"Still with me?"

Danny let out a tired grunt. "Honestly? I'm off my face on codeine. I want to sleep… on something really soft, and pretend I'm someone else for a while."

It was such an un-Danny-like thing to say. Finn folded Danny's bloodied jeans, careful to hide his shaking hands. "Do you need to keep these… for evidence, or something?"

"Nah. We've got all the evidence we need."

Finn swallowed the lump in his throat. "Who got stabbed?"

"Bob Jenkins."

"Bob Jenkins? Who's that?"

"A colleague. He's going to be okay, though. The knife missed anything that mattered."

"That's good."

"Hmm? Yeah. Yeah, that's good."

Danny looked ready to drop. Finn put his arm around him. "Your friend said you'd been discharged. How about I take you home?"

"Home? Who's at your house?"

"Everyone," Finn said. "But we don't have to go there. Your place is closer."

"Sara?"

"I'll go and get her when you're settled."

Danny nodded. "You've never been to my place."

137

"You've never invited me."

"Haven't I?"

"Nope." Finn helped Danny off the bed and into his shoes. "And it's too late to hide your midget porn collection or whatever it is you don't want me to see."

Danny turned suddenly and fixed Finn with the steadiest gaze Finn had seen from him so far. "It's not that. It was never that. My place is just… nothing, you know? I'm never there."

"Looks like you need to be there now. Come on. Let's go."

DANNY'S FLAT was ten minutes down the road. They made the drive in silence, and then Finn took Danny's keys from him and let them in.

"Do you want a shower?"

Danny nodded. "Yeah. I can't get my stitches wet, though. Make yourself at home, okay? I'll be back in a minute."

Finn gazed around as Danny sloped off to the bathroom. Danny's flat was everything he'd said it was: clean, sterile… nothing. It felt like no one had ever lived there, let alone anyone as warm and sweet as Danny.

He put his boots by the front door and hung his coat up. Then he looked around for something for Danny to eat before he inevitably crashed out.

Danny's fridge was bare bar some dubious-looking cheese and a lonely egg. There was milk for tea, though. Finn made a strong brew and went looking for Danny's bedroom. He found it neat and tidy like the rest of the flat, and sat down on the bed to wait for Danny.

He didn't have to wait long. Danny emerged from the bathroom a few minutes later, moving slowly, with his arm wrapped around his torso and his face creased with pain.

Finn jumped up and took his weight. "Come on. Get into bed. I'll get you some more painkillers."

With Finn's help, Danny pulled on a pair of jogging

bottoms and lay down on his uninjured side, head propped in Finn's lap.

Finn played absently with Danny's hair. "Do you want to talk about it?"

"About what?"

"What happened to you."

"Nothing happened to me, Finn. One minute I was with you, the next I was arse-over-tit on the pavement with my head smashed in. I'm not the one who got stabbed or strangled and dumped by the roadside."

Finn stilled his fingers. "Do you wish you were?"

If Danny thought the question odd, he didn't show it. He shook his head slightly and closed his eyes. "No. I just wish we'd caught him sooner."

"You've got him now, though, right? The news said he was under armed guard in hospital. Did he get hurt?"

"We got hit by the same car. Bastard rolled on his own knife. He'll live."

Finn tried to picture that and cringed, glad Danny couldn't see him. A part of him wanted to know every grisly detail, but most of him was struggling to cope with the very real notion that a few seconds either way could've taken Danny away from him forever. "What happens now?"

"Now we have to make sure the case against him is watertight. He's got to go down, or it's all for nothing."

Danny's bleak tone alarmed Finn. "Could that happen?"

Danny shrugged a little. "If we've fucked up somewhere. The DNA evidence is pretty conclusive from Gemma's scene, at least. Now we have to prove he killed the others too, unless he confesses… shit."

Finn frowned as Danny paled. "You all right? Something hurt?"

"Nah." Danny blinked a few times. "Just remembered something I need to add to my statement. Is Sara okay?"

Finn wasn't convinced by Danny's brave face, but he let it go. What was he supposed to do? Convince Danny to fall apart? "Sara's fine, mate. I left her with Jack, remember? Will's cooking. They'll look after her."

"Does she know what happened?"

"She doesn't know about this." Finn touched Danny's forehead just below the stitched gash. "She knows about the murders, though. Will turned the telly on before I could stop him. He didn't know. I'm sorry. She was okay, though, if it's any consolation. She's a tough little thing."

"I wouldn't know. We hardly know each other." Danny sighed, and Finn waited. Danny was exhausted, but he needed to talk, even if he didn't know it. "I saw her, you know…. Sara, when we found Gemma. For a minute. I hadn't thought about Sara in weeks. Then I saw this dead, broken girl, and her face was my sister and everything I hadn't done for her."

"They're the same age, aren't they?"

Danny nodded. "Yeah, but it was more than that. It was like a sign when she turned up on my doorstep, a warning of what I'm going to lose if I don't man up and take care of her."

"You do take care of her, Danny. She told me you bought all her uni stuff. Paid for her driving lessons. Her laptop. I reckon, as older brothers go, she thinks you're pretty perfect."

Danny shook his head. "I'm not there when it matters. We fell out yesterday. She said she wanted to know me better, so I brought her to your gig."

"That's why you brought her to see me?"

"Think so." Danny opened his eyes. "You and my work… that pretty much *is* me. I don't care about anything else… 'cept maybe her. Yeah, definitely her. Fuck. I'm so bloody wasted on that codeine crap."

"You're kind of cute, all stoned and shit."

Danny smiled, loopy and exhausted. "Cute? Whatever floats your boat, mate."

"You float my boat."

"Glad to hear it." And for the first time in weeks, real happiness crept into Danny's tired gaze. He reached for Finn and tugged him down into a tight hug, the kind of hug that tied two souls together forever, like he'd never let go. "'Cause I'm a little bit in love with you."

The world—Finn's world, at least—changed forever in that moment. He kissed Danny again, a long, slow kiss, the kind of kiss that led to more... much more, but despite a rush of heat between them, Danny was asleep before Finn could pull back for air.

Finn watched him for a long moment, then covered Danny with the duvet and whispered in his ear, "I love you too. Merry Christmas."

EPILOGUE

CHILDHOOD SUMMER holidays in Newquay had always held a special place in Danny's heart. He'd learned to swim in the sea at Fistral Beach when he was six and had his first real kiss behind the cavernous rocks a decade later.

That year had been the last time Danny made the trip with his parents and Sara. After that he'd pissed off to Magaluf with his mates every summer, and the Cornish coast had faded to a distant memory. For some reason he'd never dreamed he'd go back.

And yet here he was. With the sun in his face, Danny tipped his beer bottle to his lips and closed his eyes. He'd missed most of Finn's summer tour, and he'd spent long, hot nights alone in bed dreaming of Finn, but he'd joined the tour in Bristol the day before, seen Finn headline the Big Chill festival, Jack on his DJ decks, Finn dancing around the brightly lit stage with a banjo and a harmonica. That gig had been wild and shown Danny a side of Finn he'd never seen before, but this, here and now, Finn on the rocks by the Cornish sea, the wind in his hair, just his guitar and Jack on a set of bongo drums for company… yeah, it was pretty fucking perfect.

Finn closed the show with a rhythmic take on a Nick

Drake track. Danny hauled himself from the warm sand and met him at the side of the stage. Finn jumped down into his arms, and Danny kissed him and held him tight. They were more guarded with their public affection back home, for an easy life more than anything else, but here, with sea behind them and the sun warming their backs, Danny didn't give a shit who saw him claim Finn as his own.

"That set was amazing." Danny tucked Finn's hair behind his ears. "I didn't know Jack could be so mellow."

Behind them, Will snorted, on his way to grab his own man. "He's knackered. If he'd played this gig a month ago, he and Finn would've had a punch-up."

"It's true," Finn admitted. "Dickhead drives me mental when he doesn't do what he's told."

Will chuckled and disappeared. Danny watched him go, then shook his head. "I can't imagine you punching anyone."

"Yeah?" Finn lunged at Danny, strong, agile, and beautiful, but Danny was quicker and had Finn restrained before either of them could blink. Finn laughed. "Never learn, do I?"

Danny kissed Finn's cheek. "Nope, but I like it, especially when we do this naked."

Finn smirked. Danny let him go before things could escalate, and together they made their way to Danny's patch of sun-warmed sand.

Danny sat behind Finn, arms around him, watching the sun go down until he put his head between Finn's shoulder blades and closed his eyes. Being with Finn like this, so happy and carefree, sometimes didn't feel real, like it was a fleeting dream.

Finn reached back and found Danny's hand. He understood. Of course he did. Finn understood Danny better than anyone, and he let Danny have his moment for a while. The festival was winding down, and aside from a few polite autograph hunters, most people left them alone. Danny didn't look up until Finn twisted in his arms.

"Are we ever going to talk about it?"

Talk about what? The asinine response was on the tip of Danny's tongue, but he bit it back. He'd been late joining Finn on tour because, after months of case-management hearings, Bill Hughes had finally stood trial for the murders of four young women Danny still saw in his sleep.

Finally. That was a word that didn't mean much. Danny had watched cases drag out much longer, but due to the case's high media profile and Bill Hughes's guilty plea, the court date had come through just eight months after the arrest.

Still felt like a lifetime, though. The guilty plea had meant it took a judge less than an hour to sentence Bill Hughes to fifteen years imprisonment for each murder, but the cool, calm lack of remorse for the defendant would stay with Danny forever. He didn't want it to stay with Finn too.

"It was fine," Danny said eventually. "Hughes will die in prison, and I know you know that because I was with Bigsy when he called you."

"*You* didn't call me."

"Yes, I did. I called you when I got home."

Finn scowled, though Danny could tell his heart wasn't in it. He already knew nothing on earth would make Danny talk about the horrors he and Lanes had painstakingly documented in the case files they'd handed to the CPS. About the brutal images they'd discovered on Hughes's computer when they'd searched his home. About the handwritten plans to snatch more victims off the streets. About the all too real possibility Bill Hughes had killed more women than anyone would ever know, including the fifteen-year-old schoolgirl in Finn's hometown all those years ago.

Danny's stomach churned. Unsolved murders up and down the country had been reopened to see if they could be linked to Hughes, but even without more bodies to his name, he was still the most prolific known killer of recent years.

Finn touched Danny's face and then the scar, half-hidden by Danny's hair. "Still with me?"

Danny smiled. Of course he was. "I wouldn't be anywhere else."

"Good." Finn was silent a moment, and then he let out a wistful sigh. "I wish we could stay here forever."

"Maybe we should." Danny lay back and pulled Finn on top of him. Shorts, T-shirts, bare legs. Damn, it felt good. "You reckon anyone would miss us?"

"Sara would. We could get a house with a room for her, right?"

Danny pulled a face. His relationship with his baby sister was closer than he'd ever dared imagine, but she was still twelve years his junior and pretty fucking annoying despite how endearing the growing friendship between her and Finn was to witness. "Maybe a caravan down the road."

Finn laughed. "Can you imagine? You'd have to be one of those country bumpkin coppers with wellies and a wax jacket."

"Piss off." Danny silenced Finn with a kiss. "Are we going back to the cottage tonight?"

Finn grinned. "I reckon so. Jack and Will aren't staying. They're driving to Will's dad's place tonight, so we'll have the cottage all to ourselves."

That suited Danny. Finn's close-knit bandmates had slowly but surely become Danny's friends too, but he hadn't truly been alone with Finn for weeks, and the temptation of a deserted seafront cottage was too good to pass up. "Let's go. And Finn?"

"Yeah?"

"I don't care where I am, if you're there too."

FINN PUSHED Danny down on the bed. Clothes disappeared. T-shirts, shorts, underwear—Finn was pretty sure he heard something rip, but with Danny's heated skin against him, he didn't care to look.

145

They rolled over and over, fighting for dominance, a fight Finn didn't care if he won or lost because there was no losing in bed with Danny. He was everything Finn had ever dreamed of and more, and Finn was fast growing to learn topping Danny was as mind-blowing as letting Danny turn him inside out.

Before long Finn found himself on his back, Danny covering his body from their entwined feet to their lips. Danny hard against him felt amazing, but Finn wanted more, much more. Needed more. It had been too many long weeks since they'd been naked together, and when circumstance allowed, Finn had thought of little else.

He pulled Danny down for a kiss, anchoring himself on Danny's strong neck. *I need you.*

Attuned to Finn like no other ever had been, Danny snaked a hand between them. He found Finn's cock, then his own, and jacked them together until Finn's eyes rolled. "What do you want?"

"You." Finn bit down on his lip as Danny tightened his grip. "Just you… I don't care. Just you."

Danny chuckled, low and deep. "You've always had that, mate. From the moment I saw you."

Finn opened his eyes. Danny said shit like that from time to time. Just a few little words that made Finn's heart ache in all the right ways.

He gripped Danny's shoulders and rolled them over. "I see you all the time. Even when you're not there."

The double meaning didn't faze Danny. He widened his legs and let Finn slip between them. "Show me."

Finn didn't need telling twice. He moved over Danny and pressed his lips to his throat, knowing it drove Danny wild, and felt around for the stash they'd hidden under a pillow when they'd arrived that morning.

He prepped Danny with gentle fingers, then slid inside him, watching, absorbing Danny's silent gasp and waiting for Danny to respond. Danny had fooled him the first time they'd done this, tentative and quiet, like he didn't know what he liked. Then he'd flexed his hips, once, twice, and flipped Finn over, riding Finn until Finn felt he would surely combust.

Or at least come so fast he'd never look Danny in the eye ever again.

Thankfully neither had happened, but that slow, early morning fuck had changed things between them and shown Finn a new side to his stoic, brooding lover.

Danny wrapped his legs around Finn and nudged him on with his heels. "Mmm. Forgot how amazing you feel like this."

"Yeah? What about this?" Finn rocked his hips in a biting push and slide, knowing Danny got off on a bit of rough. "Or this?"

Danny's eyes rolled. "That'll—fuck—do it. Again."

Finn obliged and fucked Danny as hard as he dared, until the only sounds in the room were harsh breaths, moans, and the bedframe hitting the wall.

Danny arched his back. "I'm gonna come."

Finn groaned with relief. Danny had always been bad for his stamina. He gritted his teeth and fought the inferno building in his belly. Danny had been jacking himself in time with Finn's cock inside him, but as Finn's hand joined his, he slowed right down, gaze locked on Finn's like neither one of them had ever been anywhere else but that moment.

Danny came with a low cry. Finn watched him unravel, then followed, startled as ever, by the bone-jarring convulsions Danny teased from him with just the scrape of his blunt nails down Finn's spine.

Finn collapsed on Danny's chest, ignoring the mess between them. His heart hammered, his limbs trembled, and he'd never felt more alive.

Danny blew warm air in his ear. "All right?"

Finn's grunt was noncommittal. Fire still burned his veins, but his muscles had deserted him and he couldn't see himself ever leaving the comforting strength of Danny's chest.

But Mother Nature wasn't so kind. Eventually the sticky mess sealing them together cooled enough to rouse Finn from his postcoital daze. He got up and floated to the bathroom for a wet flannel. He cleaned them both up and then washed his hands.

The pull back to Danny was strong... too strong to ignore for long, but as Finn turned, he glanced at himself in the mirror and smiled. The stain of the Cornish sun looked good on him, but more than that, he looked sated, content, and... happy.

About bloody time.

Finn padded back to bed. The sky had darkened while they'd been distracted, and though buzzed from an awesome gig, Finn welcomed the night and rest it would bring for both of them. It had been a long year so far. The murder case had weighed heavily on Danny. For weeks... no, months, he'd hardly eaten or slept, consumed with honing a watertight prosecution, only for the bastard to plead guilty anyway. And then, even as Danny was still caught up in evidence and hearings, the stress of the past few months had inevitably unraveled Finn's tenuous grip on his mental health.

But it wasn't all bad news. Finn's relapse had been brief and intense, but despite Finn's fear it would drive Danny away, if anything it'd brought them closer. Danny had taken a week off work, never left Finn's side, never wavered, never flinched, and Finn had emerged from a dark cloud of uncertainty feeling stronger than ever.

"What are you thinking about?"

Finn rolled onto his side to find Danny mirroring his position, watching him, like he often did, with a gentle gaze that made Finn feel safe. "I was thinking you should sublet your flat."

It was a half-truth. He'd been trying to persuade Danny to give his flat up for a while—he spent most nights a Finn's anyway, even when Finn was away—but so far Danny had resisted. *I don't want you to be stuck with me.* What the fuck did that even mean? Danny was warm and caring and kind, but he was pretty crap at telling Finn how he felt—verbally at least. Finn couldn't deny Danny's every touch and smoldering look told him exactly how Danny felt.

"Who would I rent it out to?"

Finn raised an eyebrow. That wasn't the usual vague deflection. "Um, Ben? Maybe?"

"Ben? I thought he was moving to Leeds."

"Changed his mind. More birds in Nottingham, apparently."

"Oh."

"Oh? Is that your answer?"

Danny shrugged. "Ask him. If he wants it, it's fine by me."

Finn sat up and jolted Danny off his pillow. "Do you mean it?"

"Mean it?"

"Don't wind me up."

"I'm not." Danny sensed the tone and sat up too. "Listen, I know I'm an unsociable bastard sometimes, but I love being at your place, and it feels all wrong when I'm not there, so—"

"You're gonna live with me?"

"If you'll have me."

Finn pounced on Danny, and despite the barely cooled sweat of their recent encounter, he felt like he could climb inside Danny and never come out. "I'll have you," he said when he finally pulled away. "And I hope you bloody like it, 'cause I reckon I'm never going to let you go."

Danny hummed with his eyes closed, then shook his head and laughed.

"What's so funny?" Finn asked.

Danny opened his liquid eyes and fixed Finn with that stare that made Finn's world stop turning. "Nothing's funny, mate. I just feel like the luckiest bloke in the world."

FURTHER READING

If you haven't read Will and Jack's story, you can read it in My Mate Jack.

NEWSLETTER

Get a free story!

For the most up to date news and free books, subscribe to my newsletter HERE.

This is a zero spam zone. Maximum number of emails you will receive is one per month.

PATREON

Not ready to let go of Danny and Finn? Or looking for sneak peeks at future books in the series? Alternative POVs, outtakes, and missing moments from **all** Garrett's books can be found on her Patreon site. Misfits, Slide, Strays...the works. Because you know what? Garrett wasn't ready to let her boys go either.

Pledges start from as little as $2, and all content is available at the lowest tier.

ABOUT GARRETT LEIGH

Bonus Material available for all books on Garrett's Patreon account. Includes short stories from Misfits, Slide, Strays, What Remains, Dream, and much more. Sign up here: https://www.patreon.com/garrettleigh

Facebook Fan Group, Garrett's Den... https://www.facebook.com/groups/garre...

Garrett Leigh is an award-winning British writer, cover artist, and book designer. Her debut novel, Slide, won Best Bisexual Debut at the 2014 Rainbow Book Awards, and her polyamorous novel, Misfits was a finalist in the 2016 LAMBDA awards, and was again a finalist in 2017 with Rented Heart.

In 2017, she won the EPIC award in contemporary romance with her military novel, Between Ghosts, and the contemporary romance category in the Bisexual Book Awards with her novel What Remains.

When not writing, Garrett can generally be found procrastinating on Twitter, cooking up a storm, or sitting on her behind doing as little as possible, all the while shouting at her menagerie of children and animals and attempting to tame her unruly and wonderful FOX.

Garrett is also an award winning cover artist, taking the silver medal at the Benjamin Franklin Book Awards in 2016. She designs for various publishing houses and independent authors at blackjazzdesign.com, and co-owns the specialist stock site moonstockphotography.com

Connect with Garrett
www.garrettleigh.com

ALSO BY GARRETT LEIGH

27697124R00099

Printed in Great Britain
by Amazon